Jarod
and the
Mystery
of the
Joshua Trees

A National Park Adventure Series Book

Jarod
and the
Mystery
of the
Joshua Trees

Janice J. Beaty

SUNSTONE
PRESS

SANTA FE

Sunstone books may be purchased for educational, business, or sales promotional use.
For information please write: Special Markets Department, Sunstone Press,
P.O. Box 2321, Santa Fe, New Mexico 87504-2321.

Cover illustration and drawings by Lillian C. Beaty
Book and cover design › Vicki Ahl
Body typeface › Maiandra GD
Printed on acid-free paper
∞
eBook 978-1-61139-339-2

Library of Congress Cataloging-in-Publication Data

Beaty, Janice J.
  Jarod and the mystery of the Joshua Trees : a National Park adventure series book /
by Janice J. Beaty.
       pages cm
  Summary: "Ten-year-old Jarod, an indigo child with psychic abilities, goes camping with
his sixteen-year-old brother in Joshua Tree National Park and finds the park desperately
needs their help, which they, after exciting adventures, provide"-- Provided by publisher.
  Includes bibliographical references.
  ISBN 978-1-63293-037-8 (softcover : alk. paper)
  1. Joshua Tree National Park (Calif.)--Juvenile fiction. [1. Joshua Tree National Park
(Calif.)--Fiction. 2. Brothers--Fiction. 3. Psychic ability--Fiction.] I. Title.
  PZ7.1.B4344Jar 2015
  [Fic]--dc23
                                        2014038434

WWW.SUNSTONEPRESS.COM
SUNSTONE PRESS / POST OFFICE BOX 2321 / SANTA FE, NM 87504-2321 /USA
(505) 988-4418 / ORDERS ONLY (800) 243-5644 / FAX (505) 988-1025

To:

Ann, Marigold, & Max
A Terrific Team

Preface

I love our Southwestern National Parks, especially Joshua Tree National Park in the California desert. But I was as surprised as the characters in this story to learn how mysterious the trees and boulders and "critters" in that park could be. In fact, many of the strange coincidences with the roadrunner, coyote, trees, and rocks actually happened to me while I was in the park. I knew I had to write a story about them. The characters, ten-year-old Jarod and his sixteen-year old brother Darrell, came from my own sons and the camping we did long ago on the Outer Banks of North Carolina in our own orange VW camper bus. "You better believe it!" as Darrell would quip if he were here. Go see for yourself, I would add.

Once I have thoroughly researched an area—its animals, plants, weather, and its problems, I turn on my computer and the writing takes off. What was surprising to me about this story was the fact that as I wrote, I learned new things about Jarod and his brother I didn't even know or plan to include. "Whoa!" as Darrell would retort. Writers don't always have control of their characters, you know, and I surely didn't with these two. Read it and see for yourself.

Coincidences galore always occur to me as well as to my characters. When I wondered if I should include an orange VW camper van from the 1970s in a story taking place in 2010s— whatdayaknow, a beautiful vintage orange VW bus actually pulled up next to me at a gas station in New Mexico! So the bus is in and it's orange!

I wrote this book for middle school readers like those I taught in Upstate New York and Guam in the Pacific many years ago. But it's really for everyone—to get caught up with and help to preserve the glory and the grandeur of our National Parks. So go out and visit one!

—Janice J. Beaty

1

Where's the Trees?

Hi! My name is Darrell Freeman, but you can call me Darry like everyone does. Just so you don't call me Deary like my ten-year-old brother Jarod. I'm sixteen, old enough to get a driver's license, which I have, but not as old as I want to be, if you know what I mean. I'm tall enough to be taken for eighteen, which I sometimes am. That's okay if people want to think that. I didn't say it. Our family doesn't believe in lying. And that goes for Jarod, too. But he certainly tells some stretchers.

Anyway, this story isn't about me. It's about Jarod. "Jay-Rod," I call him, which he hates. Jarod will probably always be the center of any story because of his "abilities," as Mom calls them.

What are they? Well, he can see things and hear things that nobody else can. So what? I can do the same. Just try me. I can tell you all sorts of things I see and hear, and if they're invisible, then who can prove it? I know. Mom always believes Jarod and not me. That's okay. I don't have the imagination for it anyway.

My mom is a painter. Well, an "illustrator," as she says. She illustrates books and magazines and has her own gallery in our house, where she sells her "illustrations." She paints scenery mostly, and trees. Trees are her specialty. She has painted every tree in Florida where we live, I bet. Palm trees—did you know there are hundreds of different kinds of palm trees? And pine trees and banyan trees with a hundred trunks, and strangler figs. I really like that kind. You know it.

Maybe Mom's tired of Florida. I don't know. But all of a sudden she is packing us up in our vintage orange VW camper bus and driving us all the way out to California, where there are really "some kind of trees," she says. But we don't quite make it all the way, at least to the kind of trees I had in mind. You know, those humungous thousand-year-old redwoods and sequoias. We sort of take a detour at Twenty-Nine Palms, California (that's a town, ya know), and turn into Joshua Tree National Park. Another desert! I was prepared to be bored to death.

So here we are at the Visitor Center and Mom is buying tree books and rock books and maps and things. I'm looking around for something to eat. And Jarod is outside seeing what kind of critters he can scare up. Oh, he doesn't have to scare up anything. They just naturally come to him. You know how rabbits scoot away at the drop of a potato chip? Not from Jared. They hop right up and look him in the eye. And birds. Why, he can whistle almost any bird's call and it will fly right up and sit on his finger. What is he? Some kind of Francis of Assisi? (I don't know what that means. My mom says it)

Omygosh! Just look at him. There he stands next to this huge fuzzy old cactus with a bird on his head! And it isn't just standing there either. It's trying to hop around and peck his hair, and all the time chuck-chuck-chucking. Whoa! It's going to get all tangled up in that curly red mop he won't let anybody cut..

"Hi, Deary," he burbles at me. "Look what I've got! A cactus wren! Isn't she cool? Think she might procure a piece of my hair for her nest?"

"Procure, doughcure!" I burble back. "He's looking for bugs, and I think he found a big one! Look out!" But before either of us can pursue that little chat any further the bird takes off and darts into a nearby tangle of cactuses.

"All right, boys. All aboard!" Mom hollers. "We're ready to take off for another adventure. Keep your eyes peeled for roadrunners! First one to see one gets a prize!"

She is always saying that since we got to the Southwest. They're those weird cartoon birds that run along saying beep-beep as they're being chased by wily coyotes, don't ya know. But we've never seen one. Just like in Florida when we're driving along, she says: "Keep your eyes peeled for alligators. First one to see one gets a prize." I'm not sure I want to find out what my mother's prize is, knowing her sense of humor. It might end up being to put up the tent, or haul firewood, or maybe even feed the alligator!

Anyway, I don't even think roadrunners are real. I think she just says that to keep us occupied so we don't tease each other all the time. We have a cartoon outline of a roadrunner she stenciled on both front doors of our camper bus, but that's all. She calls our bus "Roadrunner II" because it's the second VW camper bus we've had.

I love this bus, but I also hate it. It's great for travel because it has a table that folds out in back of the front seats for playing games, and a little refrigerator for snacks, (yum-yum), a sink and stove, and a long back cushioned space where you can stretch out and snooze. And of course, a poptop which pops up above the roof at night for sleeping, and a tent which you put up outside, attached to the sliding side door. Jay-Rod and me "trade" (fight over) the poptop and tent for sleeping spaces and Mom sleeps in back.

But I also hate this bus for being orange...orange, can ya believe it? So everybody laughs at us and calls it a "hippie wagon," which it is not. We may be weird, but we're not hippies (whoever they are).

So now we are on our way again. I'm in back sitting on the long seat behind the table while Jay-Rod is up front helping Mom navigate. (What's to navigate, I wonder? There's only one main road through the whole park!) Anyway, he's following the map and looking out the window at the same time, very intense like he gets, and excited about every little thing. What's to get excited about? I don't see a thing but desert and a few rocks. Not even a Joshua Tree (whatever they are.)

Jay-Rod keeps making these bubbly sounds of excitement: "Eee! Uh-huh! Omygosh! Awesome! Whew! Look over there!" And finally: "Stop! Stop the bus, Mom!" And she does, carefully pulling over to the side of the road. Jay swiftly slides open the side door and is out, bounding across the desert. I don't see anything. I look at mom. Neither does she. She shakes her head and shrugs.

We both wait until along he comes with something in his hand. It is a rock. Well, that's not surprising since all there is on this desert is rocks. He passes his so-called special rock around for us to "peruse," he says. Okay. It looks just like a rock, sort of sparkly, maybe, but nothing else I can see. I shrug and hand it back.

"But don't you see it, Darry? That sparkly stuff may be gold! And can't you tell by feeling it? It has a sort of buzz to it. No, don't start up yet, mom. Let's mark this spot on the map and record the global positioning location."

"Now, Jarod," Mom warns. "You can't go keeping everything you pick up, you know. This is a national park. And I hate to disappoint you, but those sparkles look a lot more like mica to me. But tell me this: how did you spot such a small rock from so far away? We weren't even stopped.

"Didn't you hear it, Mom? Darry? It was buzzing! Pretty loud, too. I don't hear it so loud now. But if you hold it in your hand, you should be able to detect its vibration, can't you?"

"The only vibration I 'detect' is the one between your ears, Jay-Rod!" I want to throw the rock back out on the desert, but Jay quickly slips it into his collecting bag. Mom sighs and starts up the van again.

"At the end of the week before we leave, we'll return all your collectibles back to where you found them, Jarod," she tells him.

Then we go around a curve and there are the rocks—and not little ones! Whee-ew! Awesome! Even I have to sit up and take notice. Gigantic boulder piles are scattered everywhere. Some rocks are piled up as high as a six story building! It looks like God has swept out Heaven, dumped his pebbles in piles across the desert, and then forgot to clean it up. Some are dark, but most are sand-color. They're beautiful! And they sure aren't pebble-size either.

The closer we get, the bigger they get: huge, round boulders the size of a car, the size of an elephant, the size of a whale. Whoa! Some are tall and skinny. Some are short and fat. But all of them are crammed together in huge piles, like they're waiting for the next giant who comes along to cart them away.

"All right Darrell, now it's your turn to pick out a campground for us. There are several up ahead," Mom points out. We already decided we would camp in a different campground every night and explore the land around it in the daytime while she paints.

I pick Jumbo Rocks Campground because that is next up in the distance. I can see it is surrounded by gigantic boulders just itching to be climbed. But then I shout: "Wait! Wait! Let's stop here first. Wow! What is that?" There on the left side of the road is a spectacular boulder that looks like a humungous skull, half buried. And it's got two huge spooky-looking hollow eye sockets. That's for me!

"No, let's not stop there," pleads Jay-Rod. "It doesn't feel good to me, Mom. There's something not good about that rock. Let's keep going to the campground."

So she does. Wouldn't you know it? That Jay-Rod!

Then we find out that the rock is the famous Skull Rock itself. It's one of the big attractions in the park. You could tell that for sure, as we pass by with all the cars and people clustered around it. But Jay-Rod insists it is a bad place. Maybe some kind of witchcraft or black magic was done there. Wouldn't ya know it? The first interesting place I've seen, and he makes Mom pass it up.

Do you believe in witchcraft? I don't. And if you don't believe in something, it can't hurt you, I always say. I was surprised that Mom agreed with Jay-Rod, but then again, she usually does.

What neither of them knew was something I found out as soon as we stopped at the campground. There was a trail over to Skull Rock from our camp. Yup. Mom turned us loose to explore our surroundings (but no rock climbing yet, she warned). Her only other instructions were to stay within shouting distance. Great! I knew I had it made. While Jay-Rod went around hugging rocks and listening to them with his ear against the granite, I high-tailed it over to Skull Rock.

Why is it something as simple as that turns out so bad? Skull Rock was a bust as far as I was concerned. Anyway, there were too many people ooing and aahing, and trying to make spooky noises in the eye-sockets. So I came back. I could see on the map where the trail was, but somehow, I got all twisted around. Maybe I took a different trail back. I don't know. The other trails leading off here and there all looked alike. When I didn't come out at the Jumbo Rocks Campground I went back and tried again.

Now I couldn't find Skull Rock! What was going on? I tried yelling for Jay-Rod and Mom and anybody else within listening distance, but nobody answered. Where were all those people at the Rock? And then it started getting dark. Wouldn't ya know it?

Where was my cell phone? We were supposed to carry our cell phones with us wherever we went on this trip. Mine was fastened to my belt. But my belt was left behind somewhere in the camper bus. I began throwing little rocks up as high as I could and yelling. Maybe sound didn't carry down among the boulders, but someone should see a stone zinging up from them. No luck.

Well, the only thing to do was to work my way over to the biggest boulder around and try climbing it. Then maybe I could see where I was, or where Skull Rock or the campground was. Good idea. Bad move.

I know Mom had said no rock climbing today, but this was an emergency. Trouble was, I had never done any rock climbing anywhere. Believe me, it's not as easy as it looks on TV. You know it! I couldn't figure out where climbers put their feet, or what they held onto with their hands. Well, maybe a different rock would be easier. Yup. I actually scrambled and scratched my way up to the top of a boulder. But when I looked around, everything still looked the same. I didn't see anything but boulders. No people. No animals. No Joshua Trees. (What were they, anyway?) Nothing. I started yelling again, but no luck. So I decided to come down.

You know what a cat feels like that's got itself too high up in a tree? Well, that was me. I couldn't figure out how to get back down! So I sat down on the rock to think things over. What would Jarod do if he was in this *predicament* (Jay's word)? Oh, yeah, he would close his eyes and *meditate* (another Jay word). He would close his eyes and "go inside himself." I never asked him for the particulars. And then his "guides" or whoever would tell him what to do.

Did I believe any of his hocus-pocus? No. But what else was there for me to do? Did I have any guides? Probably not. But I could always try to get in touch with Jarod. Weren't brothers supposed to have some sort of genetic connection?

So I did it: closed my eyes, got calm, and tried to imagine what Jarod looked like. When his face came into my mind's eye, I sent him a mental message: "Hey, Bro, help me out. I'm up high on a rock. Gonna take my shirt off, wave it and yell. See you soon." And yippee, it worked!

Mom was mad, of course, that I took off like that; and that I went back to the Skull Rock; and that I didn't have my cell phone; and also that I climbed a boulder. But in the end I could see she was relieved I was back safe and only had a few scratches to show for it all.

Jay-Rod didn't tell her how it happened, but he told me. He said he heard me inside his head, so he just went off down the right trail until he felt which direction I was in. By then he heard me yelling.

It took some painful shinnying to get me down and we both landed in a heap, but I made it. Then he said it was the Skull Rock itself that messed me up...screwed up my directions. I don't know. Something sure happened. I won't try that again.

But Jay-Rod had something else real important to tell me. He kept hopping around and tapping on the nearby boulders.

"C'mon, out with it Jay-Rod, buddy, you're making me nervous."

It seems that while I was stumbling around the boulders, he was busily getting acquainted with them. He always got acquainted with anything new in his surroundings. I knew that. But boulders? Well, they were sure the biggest new thing around. How do you get acquainted with boulders?

According to Jay-Rod you listen to them. You plaster yourself flat against them with your body. Then you turn your head and put your ear against their rocky side. Then you listen to them. You have to keep moving around until you find the spot where their vibrations come through strong enough to be understood.

I tried not to snicker. "Okay, mister see-all, hear-all, and know-all. And what do these humungous boulders have to say to a mere mortal?"

Jay-Rod didn't even blink an eye or stick out his tongue at me. He was serious. He looked at me with those blazing blue eyes of his and spilled out this weird report: First, that all the boulders in Jumbo Rocks Campground said the same thing. They kept saying: "Sacred place. Sacred place. Sacred place."—over and over.

When he went back to the first ones just to check whether he heard it right, they had changed to saying: "Help us. Help us. Help us."

Whoa! What were we supposed to do with information like that? Did I believe it? Hard to say. But Jay-Rod sure did: that these rocks were sacred and needed help. What kind of help, I wondered? What was causing them to send out a call for help like that? Did it have something to do with the negative vibes from Skull Rock? Or was it all a bunch of hooey?

I considered my options. We could treat it as a bunch of hooey and just go on our way as before. Or we could decide there really was something true about those words and.... well. What?

Jay-Rod always seems to get information from somewhere. He says it is spiritual. He says that kids like him have come to Earth to bring new information to people: that there are big changes ahead for everyone on Earth. His information will help people to deal with it.

"Kids like him." I knew what he meant by that. Mom said he was an "indigo child." Hmm. Lots of kids born after 1982 are supposed to have different DNA and different abilities than the rest of us. I looked up "indigo" in the dictionary and it said "a shade of blue; deep blue." The only thing blue about red-headed Jay-Rod are his eyes. They're blue enough to freeze ice when he stares at you.

In the end I went along with him. Sort of. After all, mysteries are right up alligator alley for me. But how could a couple of kids help those gigantic rocks? And why did they need help? No use telling anybody else about it. They'd just laugh. In the end we didn't even tell Mom. She was too busy in the bus getting supper, anyway. We weren't around to start a cooking fire outside, so she just went ahead and used our inside stove.

But when we finished supper in the bus and came outside again (it was still light enough to see), you can't imagine what we saw. Right next to one of those cartoon birds stenciled on the door of our bus was—a roadrunner! I kid you not! A real live honest-to-gobbledygook roadrunner with its long tail and raised head crest! Awesome! And it wasn't a bit scared of us.

My mouth was hanging open. Mom didn't know what to think. But ol' Jay-Rod was just grinning all over. He said he got the bird to come here, so he deserved the prize. Right. Mom handed him a bag of trash to take over to the garbage bin! See what I mean?

But first she gave him a big hug as the bird scampered off into the bushes. Beep-beep! And still no Joshua Trees!

2

Split Rock

Good morning! It's great to be in Joshua Tree Park after all! The weather is so bright and fresh and not a bit like humid Florida. We pile out of sleeping bags, and the first thing we always do on our trips, even before we finish breakfast, is to ask Mom: "Are there any messages?" We don't mean cell phone messages, but messages on her laptop that she often writes for us after we're asleep, to be read in the morning.

Sometimes they're serious, sometimes silly, and sometime just plain weird. Sometimes she makes us learn a quote by heart. (Jarod is home-schooled, ya know, because he's ADD, can't sit still in a regular classroom, and anyway, the kids always pick on him.) So I have to learn the fallout from his lessons, too.

Mom revs up the bus motor, plugs in her laptop, and takes a look. "Oh, yes," she says, pretending to be surprised. "Here's one for Jarod."

By and by, in the bed of a shallow rivulet, I found a deposit of shining yellow scales, and my breath almost forsook me! A gold mine!

I asked my partners to cast their eyes on that and tell me what they think of it

"Think of it?" said old Ballou, the miner, "It's nothing but a lot of granite rubbish and nasty glittering mica!"

Moralizing, I observed then, that all that glitters is not gold. Mr.Ballou said I could go further than that, and lay it up among my treasures of knowledge: that nothing that glitters is gold! That gold in its native state is but dull, unornamental stuff, and that only lowborn metals excite the admiration of the ignorant with an "ostentatious" glitter!

"Ha!" I say smugly, looking over at Jarod. "How come you didn't know that, smarty-pants? I bet you don't even know who said it."

"Mark Twain," he replied without blinking an eye. "Mark Twain in *Roughing It* when he went West with his brother on a stagecoach after his Mississippi steamboat was closed down by the Civil War."

"Very good, Jarod," said Mom, approvingly. And what did *you* learn from that quote, Mr. Darrell?"

"Os-ten-ta-tious. That lowborn mentals like Jarod are always glittering ostentatiously!" Jarod threw his breakfast muffin at me, but I ducked and it sailed out the side door and into his tent. "Crumbs for the roadrunner! It's my turn in the pop-top tonight!" I yell.

And so we were ready for another day in this peculiar national park—on our way to see the famous Split Rock. While Mom got her painting things together in back, she let me drive for a change. Now I was forced to view the landscape with more than a passing glance. Whoa, what are those strange plants with all the twisted arms that seem to be growing all over? Mom had me slow down.

"Those, Darrell Freeman, are what you have been complaining all the time about not seeing, and what we came here specifically to see. Those are Joshua Trees!"

"Whoa! Who'da believed it! What weird beasts! They don't even look like trees. Why are their arms—their branches, with those spiky green things at the ends—why are they growing every which way? They look drunk or deformed or something."

"The Mormon pioneers didn't think so," Mom replied. "You need to remember the Joshua Tree is the biggest plant on the Mohave Desert, and when the Mormon pioneers were struggling across what they called the Great American Desert, they were happy to see anything that resembled a tree. They thought it looked like the prophet Joshua in the Bible pointing them the way to the Promised Land. So that's what they named the tree."

"It's a giant yucca plant, silly," spoke up Jarod, finally coming to life in the back of the bus, "like the Spanish Bayonet plants we have back in Florida. You always thought those were pretty cool, didn't you?"

"Yeah, until I got stabbed with the end of one. But these trees are so weird-looking. Well, maybe you could imagine they're Spanish dancers." I took my hands off the wheel for a second, raised my arms up, and gyrated around in my seat like a flamenco dancer until Mom gave me a swat.

"Every single Joshua Tree in this desert is different from every other one!" Mom exclaimed. "I love them! I think they represent the most violently freedom-loving life in the entire plant kingdom. And I am going to paint them all!"

"Uuuuuh!" is the sound that came out of my mouth.

"Yippee!" cheered Jarod, and started doing a violent freedom-loving-Joshua-Tree dance in the space between the table and the back seat.

"Hey! You're rocking the boat!" I yelled, swerving off the road and coming to an abrupt stop. "How come you're getting him all worked up, Mom? I thought you wanted me to help keep a lid on the kid." (Jarod tends to go to extremes whenever he gets excited).

Now he slid open the sliding door, hopped out of the bus, and took off into the desert, twirling around like an Apache doing a war dance. (Yeah, I know. Not politically correct words. But it sure describes his movements). I watched in wonder as he stopped in front of every nearby Joshua Tree and did a dance for it, spinning around and waving his arms above his head just like the tree branches in front of him.

That was too much for me. I had to get into the act too. I hopped out and started whooping and pounding out a crazy rhythm with the flat of my hands on the side of the bus. A couple of cars pulled up behind ours and started taking pictures of us whirling dervishes and the trees. Then a few more stopped. Hey, Mom had her camera out too!

When it was all over, our impromptu audience clapped, waved, and went on their merry way. Whew! What was all that about?

Finally Jarod came back and started telling us this wild tale about the Joshua Trees talking to him. They told him how they had been much freer in the beginning and able to move about and "dance" in the wind. Oh, yeah, I'll bet.

And the first Native Americans danced with them in their ceremonies. After awhile things got denser, they told him, and they got sort of frozen in the positions they now hold. Just like kids in the game of statues. (Did you ever play that?)

"It's like they are an enchanted forest of dancing trees," exclaimed Jay-Rod, "frozen in place."

Now, what do you say to a little brother who tells you things like that? Was it his imagination or what? To him it was as real as talking to me. I asked him how he heard them "talk" and he insisted he heard it in his head just like he heard my call for help yesterday.

So then I finally asked him, what words did you actually hear me say in your head, and he repeated them exactly: "Hey, Bro, help me out. I'm up high on a rock. Gonna take my shirt off and wave it and yell." I told him he left out the last part. He thought a minute and said, "Oh, yeah: 'See you soon.'" I shook my head in wonder, got back in the bus, and let Mom drive.

"And there's something else," added Jay-Rod mysteriously, cupping his hand and whispering in my ear. These trees feel just like the rocks. Like they're trapped. Like something's going to happen and they can't get away. They want help. And they think we can help them… well, me, I guess they mean. They think I can help."

Whoa! What kind of place is this, anyway? We've traveled and camped in almost every campground up and down the East Coast, but all their rocks and trees kept their mouths shut!

Maybe it was Jay-Rod. Maybe he was developing some more of his weird "abilities." Every once in awhile he came up with some new off-the-wall stuff. Mom said it was because he was maturing. Some indigo children don't show their "indigo-ness" until they're almost grown. Uuuh!

So what were we supposed to do? I knew that if Jay-Rod was the one that these harebrained rocks and trees had picked to do their dirty work, I'd have to go along, too. Because if you just turned Jay-Rod loose without any limits, no telling what he'd do or where he'd end up.

"Well, what do they want you to do? Bring in the Marines?" Of course, he didn't know. And how was he going to find out? "Ask them," he said.

Them? Them? All of those millions of boulders piled up like cannonballs on God's battlefield? And all of those crazy Joshua Trees engaged in their dance contest for statues?

Jay-Rod was silent for a change. I know you don't hear him say very much, because I only report the teeniest fraction of his burblings. If I said them all, this story would never end.

Oh-oh, he was going into himself again. Sometimes that lasted longer than you'd want to know about. But suddenly he came out of it.

"No," was his answer.

"No, what?" I asked.

"No, not all of them. Ask only one. One rock and one tree. We have to ask the right rock and the right tree. You and me. Both of us. We're both involved. They think that kids like us can do this better than adults."

Do what? Help them? How in the whacky world d'ya find the right rock and the right tree, anyway? Wait a minute! Where did this "we" come from? I know I said I'd keep an eye on Jay-Rod, but how did I get mixed up in his deal with the wacko native "residents" of this park? Was I supposed to go around and start interviewing every rock in sight?

"Knock! Knock! I say there, old chunk, how's it going with you today? Any chips off the old block?" Uuuuh!

Things were getting pretty *ostentatious*, it seemed to me!

"Boys! Boys!" This from Mom. "Are you keeping track of the map? We're supposed to be on our way to Split Rock, remember. There's a turnoff around here somewhere.

Yep, there it was. We almost missed it. You could see Split Rock from the turn-off. We drove up to the parking lot, got out, and climbed up a path to the gigantic boulder. It really was split in two from top to bottom. Oh-wow! It was humungous! Would this be the rock that would give Jay and me our secret instructions? I pretended I wasn't excited about finding out, so I read the guidebook to Mom about how rock outcrops like this were formed. Jay-rod, of course, rushed off to commune with the rock itself.

The book told how this rock was formed underground millions of years ago. While still underground it eroded into its rounded shape till it was finally pushed up into an outcrop. But the strange thing that none of the geologists can explain is the split. The split does not show any eroding or weathering, so it must have been cracked while on top of the Earth by something else.

Lightning? Maybe. An earthquake? Could be. No one knows. The guidebook said that visitors have even suggested supernatural forces or UFOs. Oh-wow! Imagine a serious guidebook mentioning such things. As I said before, this is a weird place.

There was Jay-Rod, working his way around the rock by flattening his body flush against it here and there, arms outstretched, and then turning his head to listen with his ear against the rock. People at a nearby picnic table were pointing to him and making sarcastic comments like "What'd'ya hear? What's it telling you, kid?" Then they looked in my direction to see if he belonged to me.

"He's just measuring the rock for a science project," I informed them.

"C'mon, Jay-Rod," I whispered to him. "Let's go, or people will think there's something wrong with you." He didn't pay me any mind, of course, and went right on with his hugging. So I said in a loud voice: "How high do you think it is? Maybe 30, 40 feet? And it's supposed to weigh over 130 tons, isn't it? Hmm. What are you getting for its circumference?"

I could tell he wanted to squeeze inside that crack but he didn't get very far. To me it was just another big rock. Yeah, it looked neat and all, but so what? Because it had a mysterious split in it, they named it and made up stories about it, just to draw in the tourists.

There were thousands of boulders just like this one in the park, but without splits. Mom even had a book on "bouldering"—climbing the boulders—that named hundreds of them and rated them for their difficulty of climbing. Joshua Tree National Park is a rock climber's paradise. You know it!

I loved the names. Imagine climbing up boulders named Turtleface, Soft Pretzel, Trash Can Rock, Lobster Lieback, Rats with Wings, Terminator, Attractive Brunette (that one's for me!), and Slam Dunk! I kid you not. They're in the book. Was I still into rock climbing? After my last adventure and the unhealed scrapes up and down my front, I would have to think it over. Slowly.

Mom set up her easel down on the desert below the rock and started painting a scene. The people left the picnic table next to the rock, so I sat down to wait for Jay-Rod. When he finally joined me, he had the queerest look on his face. It was like: I know something that you don't know, but I don't know if I should tell you.

"Okay, okay, Bro, out with it!" I wheedled. "I know you're hiding some deep dark secret."

Long pause. Then it came out: "Darry, I heard it all! The whole story! You're not going to believe this! No one is! I know what the rock's doing there! I know how it got split! Wow! It is a deep secret. An underground secret. Another long pause. "This happened so long ago—eons ago—the rock hardly even remembers it."

Wait a minute. Rocks have memories? This was too much!

Jay-Rod sort of picked up on my thought. "Of course they do. Rocks have long memories. They're alive like I've been trying to tell you. Everything on Earth is alive—all of God's creatures—even grass and trees—and water and wind. But they're not three-dimensional like us, or becoming four-dimensional.

"That's why we have trouble understanding them and thinking they're not alive like us. But they are. Maybe not like us, but alive. Rocks are one-dimensional, you know. And when I listen to them very carefully I can just about make out what they have to say.

"Split rock was once a whole rock, unbroken. It 'lived' up there on top of one of those huge rock piles. Way up there, see? And where it's standing now was once an opening into the Earth. It was sort of a tunnel that went deep, deep down through the rocks into another world—where people made themselves an underground city.

"When the people had their underground world ready to live in, they sealed it off at the tunnel opening up on Earth by dropping that gigantic rock to cover the opening. That's what cracked it—when they dropped the rock. I guess there must have been other people on Earth that wanted to get down there too—maybe to harm the underground people. They even tried to squeeze through the crack, but they never made it."

Oh, man-o-man! This takes the whole chihuahua, if you know what I mean. Jay-Rod has told some pretty huge whoppers, but this humungous rock tale tops them all. What was I supposed to say? To humor him I finally said he better keep the story to himself so some other scheming people don't try to find the opening.

He looked at me sort of funny and reminded me about the underground city under Mt. Shasta in California that we both read about in one of his science fiction magazines. Maybe this was another entrance to that, he figured.

Still, this story had nothing to do with what the other rocks or trees had told him. At least it didn't seem too. It wasn't asking us to help or anything. Then I had an idea. If he could actually hear something by pressing his ear against the rock, why couldn't we press the mike of a tape recorder against the rock and see what it would pick up.

Uh-uh, he said. The vibrations would be too low and slow for any tape recorder to pick up. This sound was very deep, and it took his brain a long time to pick up and translate the sounds. He had to go round and round the rock until he found a place where the vibrations came through strong enough. And they weren't really words, anyway. More like "thought-feelings."

Okay. But how could those underground people lift the huge Unsplit Rock in the first place, I wanted to know, and then drop it over their tunnel entrance when they were already inside?

You know Jay-Rod had that answer, too. He always does. "Listen, Deary," he said like he was talking to a kindergartner, "Those first people had powers like you wouldn't believe. Look at the gigantic stone statues on Easter Island, the millions of huge stones in the Great Pyramid, and even Stonehenge. You don't think the people carried them there with their bare hands, do you? They were super-duper stone movers. They moved them with their minds, and also with the sounds they made.

"I can almost see them climbing up to Unsplit Rock on top of the pile where it lived and making a big circle around it," he explained. "First they would ask its permission to move it. Then they would meditate very deeply. And finally they would all make the same sound—a certain tone, for a long time. Then they would retreat to their tunnel.

"When the time was right, they would call the stone with their sound and direct it with their minds. When it was exactly over the opening, they would suddenly stop the sound so the stone would plunge directly into the mouth of their tunnel and plug it up.

"But I think they misjudged the force of that gigantic boulder. When it hit the solid rock walls of the tunnel, it split completely in two. Look at Split Rock, Darry. You can see that there's got to be as much of that rock underground as above. It's not just sitting there on top of the ground. It's plugging up a hole."

Whew! I was going to say that geologists could use sounding devices to find out how much of Split Rock was underground, when I stopped short. What was the use? Jay-Rod had little use for modern science. In his mind it's too narrow and limited in its thinking. New ideas are usually shot down. The people who think them up in the first place usually lose their reputations and even their jobs for their trouble.

All I could think to say was: "You better not tell Mom about this."

When we got back to the camper bus we wandered over to where she was painting. Now it was her turn to startle us. She had finished a brand new work: *surrealistic*, she called it. No tree this time, but an x-ray version of Split Rock, showing the rock and its split going deep into the Earth, and radiating energy out of it like rays from the crash of a meteorite hitting the Earth. I kid you not. "Omygosh!" was all I could say.

3

Joshua Trees and SUVs

"Slower! Drive slower!" yelled Jay-Rod to me as we zipped along the road through the park. Mom wanted to paint back at the campground so for once she allowed me to drive through the park on my own. I had to promise to stay within the speed limits and to call her on my cell phone every hour on the hour to tell her where we were.

We also had to stay on paved roads only and not take off on any gravel roads no matter how tempting they looked. "Break the rules, and you lose the keys," she warned.

I guess she decided we couldn't very well get lost even if we followed some of the paved branches off the main road, since they were dead ends and we'd eventually have to back-track. She knew Jay-Rod would tell on me if I did break the rules.

I was in my glory anyway to be in command of our orange-marmalade bus. One hand on the wheel and one out the window waving, I sang out every verse I could make up:

Marmalade, marmalade,
Sweet or sour in the shade,
Give us more or we will fade!

"C'mon, Darry! Just because we had marmalade muffins for breakfast, do you have to announce it to the whole world? People will think there's something wrong with you."

Not many people on the road, but some of them waved or shouted at us. It was a great day. The Joshua Trees scattered here and there on every side stretched away to rock piles in the distance. Clear blue desert sky. Perfect temperature. And me in command! What more could ya want?

Where were we going? Actually, that was up to Jay-Rod. I promised him we'd drive along till he could find a Joshua Tree that could tell him how we were supposed to help the rocks, or the park, or whatever. How was he going to do that? Not a clue. Only he could tell you.

Me? I wanted to see a coyote. We had our roadrunner experience, now we should find us a wily coyote. This time Jay-Rod wasn't so sure. Coyotes kept out of sight in the daylight, he noted. I didn't care what he said, I was going to concentrate on seeing a coyote. If he could call up a roadrunner like that, I should be able to "procure" a coyote.

Now he yelled "stop!" so I pulled over and parked by the side of a tall, thick Joshua Tree. He hopped out and went over to stand by it, staring up into its crookedy branches with their fat bunches of green daggers at the end of each. Finally he sat down on the ground, crossed his legs Indian-style and closed his eyes. Hmmm.

I don't know how long this went on since I spent my time scanning the scenery on both sides of the road for coyotes. Then another car pulled up behind us: a black SUV with tinted windows. That always happens. Did'ya ever notice?

Just because you are stopped to look at something, everyone else has to stop, too. A lady got out and walked over to the tree where Jay-Rod was sitting. I don't think she talked to him and he didn't seem to notice her, but guess what? She took his picture and then left!

He finally got back in the bus. Before he could say a word, I solemnly informed him: "They got your number, Jay-Rod. Now you're going to see your photo on every Visitor Center wanted-poster. "Wanted: boy planning to plant-nap endangered Joshua Tree. Reward for information leading to arrest: 50 cents."

Well, that joke didn't jar him in the least. But it got us thinking. Why would that woman take his picture and not the tree's? Were we, maybe, being followed? Did someone know about Jay-Rod and his abilities? Had he stumbled across something important that someone wanted left alone? Maybe the entrance to the underground world?

We tried to remember whether we had seen that SUV before. Maybe at the Split Rock parking lot. Hadn't it been parked next to us? Naw, it's just our imagination, I decided. Let's not get off track. What I really wanted to know was what the Joshua Tree said to Jay-Rod.

"Nothing,"

"Nothing? Then what took you so long?"

"I was waiting for it to say something. But all I heard was some sighing in the wind. It sounded sad. I guess it wasn't the right tree."

"Maybe you should do one of your violent freedom-loving Joshua-Tree dances for it," I offered. Jay-Rod scowled.

So that was the way the day went. I'd stop for Jay-Rod at some different-looking tree. He'd hop out and go meditate in front of it. Then he'd hop back in and report: nothing. This was getting boring. So I finally turned around and headed back to the campground for lunch.

What a surprise awaited us! There, four campsites over from ours, an SUV was parked. You guessed it: the black SUV with the tinted windows! Mom had been off painting when it arrived, and now nobody was around. She thought they were probably rock climbers and would be gone the rest of the day. I looked at Jay-Rod and he looked at me. We just shook our heads.

After lunch we both asked Mom if we couldn't change to a different campground, but she liked this one. Why? She wanted to know. Everything was so convenient here: picnic table in the shade of a big boulder, restroom not too far away, privacy with few campers around, and wonderful rocks with Joshua Trees to set them off. Just right for her painting. She had just started a new scene, so she wasn't about to leave now. She wanted us to give her one good reason why we should move.

I said there were people too close to us. She just scrunched up her face and shook her head. Jay-Rod said: "Too ostentatious." That really got to her and she laughed.

"Okay. Tell you what we're going to do. You go off and do your driving, and I'll finish my painting. And by the way, you forgot to check in on the cell phone, Darrell. Don't forget this afternoon. Come back by four pm and we'll go look for another campground.

So we were off again. I stopped for so many Joshua Trees, I quit counting. But I couldn't help but look over my shoulder for any black SUVs. Not a one.

Finally I decided we were running out of trees. They don't grow everywhere in the park. There was only one of any size in the desert on either side of us, and it was pretty scrawny. Tall enough, but not very thick with only a few dagger leaves or whatever you call those green spikes. I guess it was pretty old. Some of them live 800 years, Mom said.

I shouldn't have pointed it out to Jay-Rod, because of course he had to check it out. So out he hopped and jogged over to it.

Pay dirt! He was yelling at me to c'mon over. All right. Just this once. Then he wanted me to listen. Well, you know what I heard: nothing! Just the s-s-swishing of wind through its branches.

But Jay-Rod couldn't have been more excited! He said all the trees' words started with an "s" sound: "s-s-s-s." But this one said something more: "s-s-standing s-s-stones." If you listened really closely you could hear it.

Standing stones? What in the yucky universe are standing stones? Of course, Jay-Rod knew. How does he know all these things even in places he's never been in before? Standing stones are large boulders that stand upright and apart from the rest of the boulder piles.

Okay, if you say so, I decided. Is Split Rock a standing stone? Yes, he said. How 'bout Skull Rock? Yes. He said there were lots of others in the park, but he didn't know their names. So how were we to find the right one? Or would any of them do? Or would we know the right one when we found it? He didn't bother to answer.

Oh, great, I muttered. Here we go again on another wild rock chase through the park! Make way for the marmalade bus!

Just then my cell phone rang. It was Mom, of course, who wondered where we were. It was after four o'clock, she said, so she guessed we'd stay put at the campground another night. I asked if the people with the black SUV were still there. She said they'd left before she got back to our camp from her painting expedition. Hmmm.

Well, maybe we didn't need to worry about them after all. Then a black SUV passed us and seemed to slow down. Wouldn't you know it. Was it them? It gave me the jitters. Jay-Rod laughed at my worrying. How many black SUVs do you think there are in this park, he wanted to know.

Okay, I would count them all. But of course that didn't work because some would pass us one way and then come back the other. At one trail site parking lot I counted three, or was it four? And when we came back down the trail after a quick look around, there was only one, a familiar one, I think. I wrote down its license number just in case.

Should we go back to our campground? We still had about two hours before sunset. I called Mom and told her we'd stay out till then. We were on our way again, this time looking for standing stones. Even if there wasn't any message, just being on the trail of a mystery was great. I rolled down the window and shouted to the world:

Marmalade bus, marmalade bus,
Here come the kids in the marmalade bus!
That's us!

Now Jay-Rod seemed to think I should keep my mouth shut if we wanted to find out anything secret without creating attention. I had to point out to him that an orange bus created its own attention with or without mouths being open or shut.

Hey, to change the subject, what's that ahead of us in the road, I wanted to know?

Directly in front of us in our lane some strange pale-looking creature was rolling over and over. Had it been hit by a car or was it just scratching its back? I put on the brakes and pulled up sharply. It stood up, shook itself, and turned to give us a big stare.

Omygosh! A coyote! I kid you not. Just like Jay-Rod and his roadrunner, I had called up a coyote! Even Jay-Rod was impressed. Well, was it just going to stand there and stare at us? I honked the horn, but it didn't move a muscle.

"Here we are, ol' boy. Now what? We got you here, or you got us here. What's it going to be?"

I was leaning my head out the window and shouting. But no movement on his part. I thought these wild critters were scared of people. What's going on? Then very deliberately it pranced across to the side of the road and kept going. Suddenly it turned off onto a side gravel road just ahead. Of course, I followed.

Jay-Rod was beside himself, jumping up and down in his seat, trying to keep track of the coyote, at the same time reminding me of Mom's warning about not going off on gravel roads.

"You're breaking the rules," he kept yelling, but in a voice that seemed to say, c'mon, let's follow him!

The coyote was trotting along faster now and I had to pick up speed. He seemed to want us to follow him else he could have turned off anywhere and disappeared into the brush. As he trotted along the road we bumped up and down and around the rock piles. Finally he stopped, turned, looked at us closely again, and really did turn off, not into the brush, but what they call a "wash," a dried up desert stream bed.

"He wants us to follow him," I shouted, pulling over and cutting the engine. "C'mon, let's go!" We both jumped out and started up the sandy wash after him. It was like he was deliberately egging us on. He could have outrun us without breaking a sweat. Why didn't he? Or why didn't he just detour out of the stream bed and up through the rocks on the mountainside?

Was he really leading us somewhere or just teasing us? It was my coyote, I decided, so I figured I'd lead the way no matter what happened. And then something did. I stumbled over a rock and fell flat out in the sand.

While I sat there a bit dazed, the coyote suddenly streaked up the mountainside, leaving us both in the dust. That didn't stop Jay-Rod, and he took off just as nimbly, over rocks and around mesquite bushes.

I got up gingerly and limped over to sit on a rock at the edge of the wash to watch the chase. They were soon out of sight. Hey, it was getting dark, I suddenly realized. I'd better check in with Mom. Come back right away, was her prompt reply.

"C'mon, Jay-Rod, let's hit the road! Forget the coyote! Mom wants us back at camp." No answer. And no Jay-Rod. I don't know how long I waited before he finally came stumbling through the underbrush and sliding down the mountainside between the boulders. He was grinning ear to ear, which meant something outstanding had happened. Yes.

"Darrell, Darrell, you're not going to believe this!" he panted. "The coyote disappeared just as I caught up with him. There he was right in front of me. Then, poof, he was gone! But guess what I found instead? A cave! And guess what was in it? Petroglyphs! You know, the ancient rock art like Mom is always telling us about. Did you know there were petroglyphs in Joshua Tree National Park? I bet Mom didn't."

"Forget the petroglyphs, Jarod. We've got to get back right away before it gets too dark to find our way back. C'mon. We can always come back here tomorrow."

"You don't understand, Bro. Petroglyphs are something special. They're ancient. They can tell stories. And guess what else? I can read them! Okay. I can see by your face you're not impressed. Let's come back tomorrow. I can also see we won't have any trouble finding the place. You've marked it pretty good with your blood sacrifice!"

"Uuuh!" I didn't realize I'd scraped my leg and it was dribbling blood down the rock I was sitting on. So I ended up limping back to the orange bus where I knew we had a first aid kit. But just as we were turning the last bend in the stream bed, we could hardly believe our eyes. There behind our bus and just beginning to turn around was the black SUV!

"They did follow us!" I yelled, suddenly regaining my strength and leaping on ahead. Of course, I hadn't locked the bus, wouldn't you know it! The two of us were in such a hurry to follow the coyote before he got away, we didn't even think of it. And now what? They were gone, but maybe, just maybe I had their license number. What did they want anyway?

Well, nothing seemed to be missing from the bus, or so I thought at first. We checked our few belongings, food, water, and maps. Most of our good stuff was back in the tent at our camp. "What about you, Jarod. You missing anything?"

Jarod looked at me real funny almost like he was going to cry. "Yep," he finally admitted. "My rock's gone."

"Your rock? What rock? We haven't been collecting any rocks."

"You know, the rock I picked up that first day. The fool's gold buzzing rock that you had such a big laugh about. It's gone."

What would anybody want with a piece of fool's gold? It wasn't real gold after all, was it? If they thought so, the laugh would be on them. Jay-Rod just shook his head in disgust. Then he muttered: "Yeah, it wasn't real gold. But maybe we could have found out what was really in it—if we'd had a Geiger counter."

A Geiger counter? Uuhhh! Uranium!

4

Petroglyphs

"Now let me get this straight, boys," Mom said, not really sure it wasn't some kind of joke. "You say you think you were being followed by people in a black SUV. That a lady got out and took a picture of Jarod sitting in front of a Joshua Tree. Well, she probably just wanted the tree and Jarod happened to be there. No? Then the black car kept turning up wherever you went. I don't know, boys. Seems to me there're a lot of black SUVs around. And you think she or somebody from that car got into our bus and took Jarod's rock? That seems pretty far out to me, too. Are you sure you didn't put the rock somewhere else? If it was so valuable to you, would you have just left it out on the seat, Jarod? And uranium? I don't think so, boys."

As you can see, Mom wasn't buying any of it. But she was interested in the petroglyphs Jarod saw. Very interested. She and my dad, when he was alive, used to go all over New Mexico and Utah during summer vacations hunting out petroglyph sites. That's where ancient people pecked out pictures on rock walls. Dad photographed them while Mom sketched them.

Did Jarod mention that he knew how to read what they said, (if he really did)? That didn't seem important enough for me to tell Mom. She probably knew how to read them, herself, anyway. She said researchers in the nearby Salton Sea area found petroglyphs that were 9,100 years old! Whoa! Ancient people had been around here that long? Awesome!

Mom did know about one petroglyph site in this park, but she had no interest in visiting it. It was ruined by movie-makers. They outlined the markings. Then they made more markings of their own just to brighten up the background for the movie they were making. How could they get away with that? I thought they fined people who defaced things in National Parks. I guess that happened before such laws were enforced. Today I bet they'd put 'em in jail.

Yup. She was very interested in seeing Jay-Rod's cave. I only hoped we could find it again. It should have been easy. We found the gravel road easy enough. But then, where was the wash that the coyote ran into? The one we thought was right turned out to be wrong right away. It filled up with rocks after the first bend and went nowhere. So we tried another. This one got wider and then branched into two stream beds. No good.

The next one had to be it. But the longer we hiked the less it seemed to lead up the mountain slope. Soon we were all three puffing as we stumbled over rocks and scuffled through sand that filled our shoes. And where was the blood-marked rock?

Mom gave up before we did. "Take me back to the campground, you boys. You're leading me on a wild coyote chase for sure." So we did.

But I was not going to give up even though Mom did. It seemed to me we needed to find out something more about what was going on. And I swear I saw that black SUV going down the gravel road again when I looked back. Maybe it was just my imagination —or jangled nerves. But nobody else had noticed it.

Anyway, I was going to put my money on Jay-Rod. If he thought that missing rock was important, then it was. After all, he had spotted it by hearing it buzz as we drove by. And if he thought the petroglyphs were important, then they were. All we were finding out in this weird park were bits and pieces of information. How did it fit together? What did it mean? We needed something more to help us figure this out.

So back we went up the gravel road to try the next wash leading off to the east. It began to look more familiar as we hiked into it.

"Hey, Jay-Rod, I see it! There's the bloody rock!"

Jay-Rod came up to the rock, sat down on it, and looked around. "I think we should have camouflaged the bus."

"C'mon, Bro, how could we camouflage a big orange camper bus like that? First of all, there aren't any trees around, just scrubby ol' mesquite. And even if we did try to hide it in the brush, somebody looking for us would be sure to spot a glimpse of that orange marmalade a mile away. A dead giveaway. We might as well leave it in plain sight, so they won't know we suspect anything.

"You're smarter than you look, Bro. You know that?" laughed Jay-Rod. "Well, up we go. Let's see if that cave is still where I left it."

It was. But it didn't look much like a cave. More like a rock shelter with an overhanging ceiling attached to a rocky wall, and several small boulders at the back almost like seats. I was disappointed in the petroglyphs, too They weren't much like the ones Mom had sketched. These were more primitive-like and smaller: all white and pecked through the dark "desert varnish" covering the ceiling. A few were white circles with smaller circles inside them.

"Concentric circles—they're suns," declared Jay-Rod. Another looked like an upside down comb with a straight line for its back and short vertical lines for the teeth. "A rain cloud," claimed Mr. Know-It-All. Several were zigzaggy vertical lines parallel to each other, and one zigzag had a definite snake head and tail rattles. "You got that right," Jay-Rod agreed.

Scattered here and there among the symbols on the shelter ceiling were little stick-figure people. They were standing with their legs apart and their arms stretched straight out, sometimes touching one another. Two seemed to be touching the ends of a rectangular grid between them. "For netting rabbits," Jay-Rod exclaimed. Whoa!

I was as excited as I knew Mom would be. Imagine, people right here in this cave making those drawings about hunting for rabbits almost 10,000 years ago!

"Hoist me up on your shoulders, Bro, so I can reach them," directed Jay-Rod. The ceiling of the shelter was higher up than I could reach, but Jay-Rod did fine on my shoulders. He directed me here and there, lightly touching each of the figures with only the tips of his fingers so as not to get them oily. (Not recommended to the public). He said he had to do it to hear what they had to say.

"Yep, I knew it. They've been here a long, long time—thousands of years. This shelter is a shaman's cave; you know, a medicine man's. He could go into trances and see things that other people couldn't, and cure diseases and such. Then when he came out of his trance, he chipped out a petroglyph to tell what happened. Yep. Okay, let me down."

Well, Jay-Rod could do that too, and without the trance business. Now he told me that the shaman was still here, (whoa! I looked around nervously), and that he had a spirit animal helper which was—guess what? A coyote! I kid you not. Now I was beginning to see where that coyote came from. Jay-Rod further explained that shamans like this often took the form of their spirit animals so they could sneak around easier to do their work. Which was?

They cured people. They warned them when an enemy approached. They showed them where to find food, water, and important medicine plants. And they protected the environment. This shaman was still doing those same things today, Jay-Rod claimed, even though he had departed Earth in his physical form.

"Oh, come on, Jay-Rod! Do you really believe all that stuff? How can he cure somebody without being here?"

"Look down at your injured leg, Bro," Jay-Rod directed.

Wow, my scrape was completely healed, the scab was gone, and even the black-and-blue bruises had vanished!

Now if he could only help us get back Jay-Rod's rock—and find the standing stone we needed to find—and tell us what we were supposed to do to help the rocks—wouldn't that be the coyote's howl!

Jay-Rod said he himself could find out more by meditating. He told me to go outside the shelter, sit on a rock somewhere, and be quiet till he came out. Then he sat down cross-legged on the floor of the shelter and closed his eyes.

I don't know how long that lasted. I just know that I was getting baked by the sun. I had to drink all the water in my canteen—so I wouldn't shrink into a little white petroglyph myself—before he finally came out. Whew!

What did he find out? Plenty: That the folks in the black SUV should be avoided at all costs. But that we would be protected from them. That we were chosen to help the rocks and trees of this sacred place because Jay-Rod had embraced them. Also because we were children and not yet infected by "the white man's disease" (whatever that is). That the standing stone was the "heart rock" and we would find it soon. That we shouldn't come back to his cave or tell people about the petroglyphs. (It's okay now, because you won't find the cave even if you look). That before we left the park we had to pay a visit to Mara (whoever that is). What about Jay's rock? Nothing.

Hoo-boy! I think Jay-Rod had really gone into a trance because the session lasted so long. Also he came out of it with his eyes sort of glassy. He gulped down water from his own canteen and shook his head several times before he came all the way back into himself. Then he could talk to me with his mouth, not his mind, and he did.

"The white man's disease was being greedy and buying all kinds of things we really didn't need instead of helping other people who did," said Jay. "Also by not respecting other people and plants, animals, birds, trees, rocks, and all the other living things around us—even bugs." Ugh.

I'm glad the shaman thought we hadn't caught the disease yet. It made me put out of my mind all the souvenirs and stuff I intended to buy at the trading post store in town before we left. Who needed them!

But who was this Mara person? Jay-Rod had no idea. Maybe Mom would know. Or we could ask at the Visitor Center. Meanwhile, we'd better get going on our search for the standing stone rock if we were going to find it before we had at leave.

So back to the bus we trotted. Well, not exactly trotted. "Trodded" would be a better word. We struggled through the sandy wash bottom and climbed around the rocks strewn through it. My leg that had throbbed painfully all the way out there was now perfectly okay. If I needed any proof that the shaman was real, I just had to look down at my healed leg.

Back at the bus I unlocked the doors and climbed into the driver's seat without a second thought. Jay-Rod hoisted himself up into his seat but let out a yell. The stone!

There was that glittering piece of fool's gold lying right in the middle of his seat! Whoa! What's going on? How did it get there? Both doors were tightly locked. I couldn't believe those SUVers would've broken back into our bus to return the stone. So where did it come from?

I looked at Jay-Rod and Jay-Rod looked at me in wonder. Was it the shaman? But how? Jay-Rod carefully put the stone into his backpack which he then placed gently on the floor between his legs. I put the key in the ignition and was about to turn on the engine when I noticed something in the road in front of us. It couldn't be, but there it was again: the coyote! There sat that same pale, shaggy beast we had followed so faithfully yesterday. We both rolled down our windows, leaned out, and cheered. Then we did a high-five so that he could see it, and I drummed out a rap on the door.

We're the kids in the marmalade bus, we are!
We've traveled through deserts so far, so far!
We drive in a bus, not a car, a car!
We know our adventure's bizarre, bizarre!
We're the kids in the marmalade bus, that's us!

The coyote pricked up its ears, pranced across the road, and disappeared into the mesquite bushes.

5

Heart Rock

Our search for Heart Rock was sure stupid now that I look back on it. Here was this huge bounty of boulders in Joshua Tree National Park strewn in piles everywhere. Some of their names suited their shapes for the tourists. Other names described their difficulty for the rock climbers. But nary a heart in the whole bunch!

We had all of Mom's park books with us: the *Geology* book, the *On Foot* book, the *Road Guide* book, the *Complete Guide* book, the *Bouldering* book, the *Rock Art Symbols* book, the *Western Birds* book, and *How Indians Used Desert Plants.* Uuuh.

It gave me a headache just to think of all that reading!

Jay-Rod, of course, didn't need to read anything. He seemed to know everything about everything just by looking at it or touching it. Why couldn't I have been born "indigo?" Just the luck of the draw, Mom said, (whatever that means).

We also had Mom's camera this time and took pictures of every rock Jay-Rod stopped to get acquainted with (you know, hug). There was Cap Rock, a flat rock teetering on top of a huge granite pile. Of course Jay-Rod wouldn't climb up that high to see if that one would talk to him. Afraid he might knock the cap off, I teased him.

We took the nature trail to see what other oddities we could see. One was a Joshua Tree that had fallen over. But it didn't fall flat—just sort of leaned over too far and couldn't get back up. Its roots were connected to the ground at one end and its top touched the ground at the other. Its bare trunk made an arch between them with only the one branch sticking straight up like a finger. We named it "One for the Money." The only thing it had to say to Jay-Rod was "s-s-s-sorry." (No, that's my little joke).

No sign of the black SUV. Should we be looking for it now that we got the rock back? I didn't want to take any chances. But the only thing I kept noticing out of the corner of my eye was some kind of bird darting from bush to bush along the trail, as if it was following us.

"Hey, another roadrunner!" Jay-Rod sang out.

Okay. No big deal. We didn't need another roadrunner experience. I told him to cut it out—to quit calling up birds and things. He said it wasn't him. Little ground squirrels also scampered up the rocks and into the crevices between them at we passed. But they were trying to escape us, not follow us.

Next we took the Split Rock Loop, a two-mile foot trail that wandered through a maze of rock piles. About a mile into the hike we came to Tulip Rock, a towering formation on top of a huge granite pile. I looked like a giant tulip flower partly closed. Jay-Rod shook his head "no." Too much effort to get up there, I guess. "Not heart-y enough," he said. I tried throwing a stone up to hit it, but it was out of my reach. Maybe that would've woken it up. But the only thing it stirred up was another roadrunner which scuttled away.

Nearby was The Tooth, a fat molar of a rock. But that didn't interest Jay-Rod either. Finally we came to a fork in the trail that took us to Face Rock, the huge stone mug of George Washington. You could climb over to that one, and Jay-Rod did. George didn't have anything to say either. But that got me to thinking about how lots of the rocks had faces that looked like people—mostly weird people. I looked around, and picked out half a dozen, very dough-boy looking faces with fat cheeks.

"You mean you just noticed that?" observed Jay-Rod, making a face at me. "I saw that when we first came in here. This park is like an enchanted garden of dancing trees frozen in place and snuffling giants frozen in stone. Maybe the faces represent real people, you know. There were giants in the Earth in those days, the Bible says."

"C'mon, Jay-Rod, enough of your weird ideas. I supposed you think you're the magician who can wave his magic wand over the place and bring them all back to life.

That got him going. He began dancing and whirling around shouting "Abracadabra, abracadabra, hokus, pokus, jingle-locus, I have spoke-us!" And throwing up handfuls of pebbles and sand in the air. I'm glad no one else was on the trail to see his craziness. But then another roadrunner darted out and disappeared again behind a rock.

So that's how our day went. We drove back and forth and up and down looking for peculiar rocks that might talk to Jay-Rod. We hiked all the shorter park trails off the campgrounds and parking lots. We saw rocks in the shapes of dinosaurs, dragons, an elephant, a manatee (from Florida), the Trojan (USC football), the Patriot (New England football), the Michelin man, and even the muffin man. But not one of them was in the mood to talk.

What finally caught our attention were all the roadrunners. Almost every place we stopped to hike had a roadrunner lurking somewhere along the way. How come we never saw any before, except the one Jay-Rod called up at our first camp?

Jay-Rod said "Is a puzzlement,"(like the King of Siam). But then he began to notice that they all looked alike. I shook my head sadly, telling him all roadrunners look alike. No, he claimed, different ones had longer tails, a toe without a nail, a broken bill, a shorter crest, brighter plumage or something. How could he tell in the brief glimpse we got before they darted away? All he said was that these birds all darted the same, too. Uuuh!

But then I had to reconsider. Jay-Rod was almost always right. So—was he trying to say that the same bird was following us everywhere we went? How could that be? We were driving in a van and a bird like that couldn't run that fast. I knew roadrunners didn't fly well. He said that maybe the bird was riding along. I argued, how could it hold on? I wasn't going that slow. (Don't tell Mom). He said maybe it rode inside. Whoa! Did he mean it was invisible?

So now we had a mystery bird just like our mystery coyote. I started making up verses and singing them loudly to the tune of *Three Blind Mice*:

Roadrunner, roadrunner,
Doesn't need to run,
Roadrunner, roadrunner,
In the burning sun;
Turns himself invisible,

Hops aboard our bus,
Tags along where'er we go,
Keeping track of us!

(Yeah, I know. Just close your ears if it's too much.)

Jay-Rod perked up, saying, "Listen to what you just sang, Bro: *keeping track of us.*
Now who said that nothing bad would happen to us? And how could he make sure it didn't
without keeping track of us? You know it: the shaman. We've got a shaman's bird riding along
with us!

Well, if that was true, wouldn't ya think the bird would just pop up now and become
visible when he heard those words? Nope. Didn't happen. But a real bird still seemed to be
following us. We had moved our camp over to Hidden Valley Campground so Mom would
have some different rocks and trees to paint, and the bird seemed to be there too. What's going
on?

Then next morning we actually came face to face with the culprit.(Jay's word). I poked my head out of the tent and shivered at first because it got cold that night. And there was a roadrunner shivering, too. Sort of flopping around, drunk-like. I was able to sneak up behind him and pick him up. "Sh-h-h-h. Take it easy, old fellow. I won't hurt you." He settled down at first but then went completely stiff like he was dead. Oh, no! Had we hit it with the bus last night?

Jay-Rod hopped down from the poptop and Mom came out to see what was happening. There I was with a dead roadrunner in my arms. But it was really okay, my bird-loving mom pointed out. The bird was displaying "nocturnal hypothermia." She told us. Huh? It is a "lethargic state" these strange birds go into by lowering their body temperatures at night when it's cold, to save energy. In the morning they need to thaw out in the sunshine before they can start running again. She told me to put it down in the sun and soon it would wake up, fluff itself out, and be fine. Whew! Neat to have a "birder" for a mom, isn't it?

While Mom went back in the bus to cook breakfast, Jay-Rod sat down cross-legged beside the bird and started meditating. I sat down too to find out what he found out. The bird "came to" before Jay-Rod did. "Hey, Bro, wake up!" By the time he finally opened his eyes the bird was long gone.

"You scared me for a minute, Bro. What took you so long?"

Jay-Rod grinned. "I was on a trip. You know, did you ever hear of 'tripping'?

"What d'ya mean? Were you in a trance?"

Jay-Rod laughed. "You could say that. When I usually meditate I don't go that deep. Maybe only to *level one* where you see geometric designs and colors and get messages. At *level two* you actually see people and animals and they talk to you telepathically. But in *level three* which is very deep you can go into the things you see. You know, walk through walls, go into coyotes, and even fly. That's what a shaman does, and that's what I did."

"Oh-wow! You mean you could really go into another person?"

"Sure," he continued. "That's what most shamans do in their trances: to find out what's wrong with sick people, why they got that way, and how to cure them. But they need to spend a long time learning how to go into such deep trances and what to do when they get there."

I looked at Jay-Rod solemnly. "Are you a shaman, Jay-Rod?" He laughed uproariously, and then told me anybody can do what he did. You just have to learn to concentrate enough to clear your mind of all thoughts, and then hold it that way for a long while. Sounds easy but it's not—unless, of course, you're an indigo.

The third level is where you go out-of-body, he said, and that's not easy for most people to do during their waking hours when their conscious self is turned on. We all do it when we're asleep, he claimed. And if you should wake up in the middle of a dream while you're still really asleep, you can do anything or go anywhere you like: walk through walls, levitate, and even fly to the moon! It's called *lucid dreaming*, he told me.

I looked at my brother differently after that. It was the first time he had revealed any of his indigo secrets. He said that within the next ten years or so, everybody would know how to tap into their inner selves like this, easily. It might even be taught in school. Oh-wow!

We are not the solid three-dimensional beings we like to think we are, according to Jay-Rod. We are really spirits made up of several dimensions. I could almost believe that because there sat Jay-Rod's solid body on the ground next to the roadrunner, while he claimed to be off on a "trip" in his *astral* body! (Whatever that is.)

And where did he go? He told me he went to the Heart Rock! Yep. He said it was a huge beautiful boulder near the road with a picnic table beside it and climbers' *pitons* pounded into its side. It was grayish granite, shaped like a humungous wedge, and taller than Split Rock. He said that the very top of it had been sliced off in ages past when earthquakes were rocking the land and boulders were flying everywhere. Awesome! Jay-Rod also knew he would able to recognize it when he saw the real thing.

Also he saw that the roadrunner was a real bird, but that the shaman's spirit had actually gone into it and directed it to keep track of us. How he got the bird to hop around from place to place like that, I'm not sure. Jay-Rod thought he actually "dematerialized" it and it rode with us—or maybe its astral body did. Sounds like science fiction to me. Now that Jay-Rod had met the shaman again, he promised to leave us alone to pursue our mission. He felt we could handle it on our own. Hmmm.

Well. All of that soon put us on the road again. We were able to find the Heart Rock without much trouble, but people were picnicking on the table next to it. So we had to bide our time till the way was clear. Finally we pulled up and parked, got out and approached the rock.

"What shall we do, Jay-Rod? You're the talking-rock expert." He felt we should each take one side of the rock, flatten our bodies against it and see what we could feel or hear. So we did. If we didn't feel or hear anything, we should shift around and do the same thing at another spot.

Believe it or not, I felt something right off! I closed my eyes, spread my arms out, and plastered myself against the rock like I was trying to hug it. It felt like it was moving! I was so surprised I almost fell over! What? I tried it again. With my eyes closed all I saw was red. But there was that motion again—back and forth, back and forth, like it was sort of rocking in place. Hey! What d'ya know? A rocking rock! I know I was supposed to be serious about all this, but you know me. I always have to lighten things up.

Jay-Rod said he actually felt the same thing over on his side of the rock! But he knew what it was: the heart of Heart Rock was beating! Omygosh! He also got the definite feeling that this great boulder of a rock was hurting and asking to be healed. Could those pitons that someone pounded in have hurt it? What was I thinking? Rocks don't have feelings! Rocks aren't alive! But somehow this one seemed to be. To me it gave off a very sad feeling—sort of a depression—like it might cry.

"Yes," claimed Jay-Rod. "It is sad. And yes, rocks are alive. I told you that before. But not alive like people are. People are three-dimensional. Rocks are one-dimensional. Very deep and very slow in their feelings. They are part of the mineral kingdom. Even scientists know that crystals are living things and keep on growing."

Okay. Okay. I wasn't going to argue with Jay-Rod. He felt that we should go back to the rock, close our eyes, put our hands flat on it, and say aloud: "Heal. Heal. Heal. Heal," and so on. I hoped no park police would come by and ask us what we were doing. I know Jay-Rod would have told them everything immediately, and they'd haul us off to the booby hatch (whatever that is).

How would we know when it was healed, I wondered? How long should we keep saying our healing chant? Jay–Rod thought I should make up a song for it. Well, I could try, I guess. I wasn't used to singing my songs to a rock. Maybe if I did one over and over the rock would understand.

What can we do for a battered boulder?
What can we do for a battered boulder?
What can we do for a battered boulder
Ear-lye in the morning?
Treat it gently till it wakens,
Treat it gently till it wakens,
Treat it gently till it wakens
Ear-lye in the morning.

You probably remember that old sailor's sea chanty: "What shall we do with the drunken sailor?" Maybe not appropriate, but better than nothing. Well, our song kept going on and on like "Ninety-nine bottles of beer in the wall," with Jay-Rod adding verses of his own. We sang: "Give it kindness in the daytime"; and "Give it kindness in the nighttime"; and "Give it lots of love and kisses"; (no we didn't kiss it!) and "Pat it softly all around it"; and "Rub sweet flowers on its surface."

By now we were walking round and round it, giving it a tap or pat now and then. Jay-Rod thought of other verses: "Christen it with a bottle of sunshine"; "Pour pure water all around it"; and "Wipe it clean with cloths of kindness." By then we were running around it (not easy to do on the back side where we had to scrunch between other rocks!) Finally, we both fell down exhausted.

"You know," panted Jay-Rod, "I can really feel something different. Something lighter. Something not so sad."

"That's because you've got this weird imagination, Bro," I wheezed. But maybe it did seem lighter.

So that was the end of that. Or so we thought. Wasn't our mission finished? Now I was trying to remember what exactly was our mission. The boulders at Jumbo Rocks Campground had whispered: "Sacred place," and "Help us." The Joshua Trees felt trapped and that we could help them. One of the Joshua Trees said to look for a standing stone. The coyote led us up to a shaman's rock shelter. The shaman told Jay-Rod that we had been chosen to help the rocks and trees, and to look for the Heart Rock. And the Heart Rock asked us to heal it. So now what else were we supposed to do?

"It's getting late, Bro," said Jay-Rod for a change. "Let's go back to the campground, have supper, sit around the campfire and tell spooky stories. After that go to sleep and dream about what we're supposed to do next."

I liked every bit of that except for the spooky stories part. We didn't need to make up anything more spooky than things already were!

6

Rock Energy

Talk about weird. That night was about the weirdest one I have ever spent! I was up in the poptop bed while Jay-Rod was down on the ground in the tent in his sleeping bag on a blowup mattress. Mom, of course, was stretched out in her own sleeping bag in the cushioned "way-back" of the bus. She never woke up.

The first thing that happened was a clunking sound on the top of the poptop. Since I was already into a weird dream, that really sent shivers up and down my spine. Finally I roused myself and tried to figure out what was happening. "Clunk." There it was again! I stuck my head out the front opening and shown my flashlight around. There was Jay-Rod outside the tent chucking stones at my sleeping quarters, trying to wake me up!

"S-s-s-st!" he hissed. "C'mon down here quick, Darry! There's someone in the tent!"

Not Jay-Rod trying to pull that old trick on me again, I thought to myself. But he kept on chucking stones, and hissing even after I turned off my flashlight and crawled back inside. So I got up again, pulled my sleeping bag around me (it was cold!), and slid down to the ground.

Once inside the tent I shined the flashlight around in the pitch-black darkness and saw: nothing. "C'mon, Jay-Rod. I don't need any of your tricks in the middle of the night!" But I flopped down on my sleeping bag anyway, and prepared to spend the night if I had to. Who knows what new-fangled idea my weird little brother had dreamed up.

"There's someone here for sure! A big someone," he whispered. "It sat on the side of my mattress and tried to roll me off! I swear! Get in your sleeping bag, Bro, lie still, and see what happens."

I did. Nothing happened—at first. Then I began to feel some very cold air make its way across my body—colder than the already cold night air. Hoo-boy! Then the cold air sat down on my feet! I kid you not. "Hey, get off me, whatever you are!" I shouted. "Hey, you're moving across my body again! Get off me! You're going to give me nocturnal hypothermia, if you don't watch out!"

Meanwhile, Jay-Rod was laughing hysterically.

This cold air had a mind of its own, for sure. It didn't move off me. Instead, I swear on a stack of Bibles, it went inside me!!! I should have kept my mouth shut. It went into my mouth and down inside me. I could actually feel its cold self investigating my insides! "Jay-Rod, help me!" I gasped, "This thing's trying to do a fast-freeze on my organs!"

But Jay-Rod didn't help. He said the same thing happened to him before he got me to come down. He said he thought the cold-air-thing was an energy form, and it was investigating us. Just like we had investigated the rocks by going around them with our bodies pressed against them.

"That was him, not me," I tried to tell it. "Jay-Rod was the rock-hugger, not me!" Well, I only did it once, at Heart Rock, I had to admit. "Get out of me, you air-bag! It's Jay-Rod you want, not me!"

What is it with the things in this weird place? Coyotes tracking us, roadrunners freaking out at our campsite, Joshua Trees engaged in a dance contest, and now a rock energy taking up residence inside us! Wait. Maybe I was still up in the poptop having a nightmare. But no, that thing was now going down inside my legs to my toes! It seemed to have filled my whole body and left me feeling slightly sick.

"Join the club!" echoed Jay-Rod.

"Do something, Jay-Rod," I pleaded, shining my flashlight at him. "Tell it to leave. Tell it we're peaceful people. We don't mean it any harm. Meditate or something."

But Jay-Rod already had his eyes closed and was going deep.

Little by little he came out with the particulars: that it was rock energy from Heart Rock; that it had followed us here; that it was old, old—ancient; that it was investigating us to see why we did what we did; that it was thankful, even happy. They all were happy—all the rocks—for the healing we did. Because he was the chief rock, all of them felt the healing. It was almost as if they had been released from some ancient curse.

All this sounds pretty crazy, now that I think back on it. But the one thing I noticed after all was said and done: it didn't leave us. That old air-bag of energy didn't go out of us the way it came in. For all I know, it's still in us! Jay-Rod says the same.

What did we do then? Wouldn't ya know it. We both fell back asleep and slept soundly the rest of the night. Mom wondered why I ended up down in the tent with Jay-Rod, since the poptop was the prized sleeping spot. But she didn't press it.

The other thing I noticed was that the rocks felt different when we drove by them or hiked among them than they had before. They seemed lighter. "Buoyant," exclaimed Jay-Rod. And happier—if a rock can feel happy.

"Look at their faces," he pointed out, "They're all smiling!"

Well, I don't know if I would go that far, but the pudgy dough-boy-looking rocks did seem to have the corners of their mouths turned-up in a rocky grin. I tried to get my brother into asking the rocks for a reward for removing the curse. But he said that would spoil the results. The release itself was the reward for everyone. I couldn't see how that was a reward for us.

He reminded me of something he was always pointing out: that we were really "mighty spiritual beings" ourselves, trapped in human bodies, but that we forgot who we were after we came to Earth ages ago. Mighty spiritual beings don't do things for selfish rewards, he pointed out.

Maybe for him, but not for me. I was still thinking in terms of the genie in the bottle. When you let it out it would grant you three wishes. I flexed my muscles, trying to feel like a mighty spiritual being, but I couldn't pull it off, driving along in the marmalade bus. If we were really trapped inside our bodies just like the rock had been, maybe it could release us, I got to thinking.

What was it doing inside our bodies now, I wondered? Was it like kryptonite that would turn us into a superman when the world needed rescuing? Hah! Fat chance! Well, I was going to pretend that it granted us three wishes, and I was going to cash in on mine when the time was right.

Right now we were driving up the road past Heart Rock, when Jay-Rod suddenly wanted to stop there again. So we did. Good. Maybe the energy would hop back into the rock and leave us forever. Nope, it didn't. But when we went over to the rock and pressed ourselves against it this time, there was a big difference. No heartbeat! It was perfectly silent with no sound or movement.

I got to thinking. Maybe the whole thing was just a dream, or a hoax, or a figment of our imaginations. But then I got to remembering that cold energy going into me, and the sick-to-my-stomach feeling I felt. That was real enough.

Once back on the road again we were heading up through a mountain pass and down into the Pinto Basin. This is one huge park, I decided. Someone said it contained seven mountain ranges. Awesome! And two completely different deserts: the Mohave with the Joshua Trees and the Sonoran with creosote bushes, jumping cactuses, and ocotillo plants. We were definitely in the Sonoran Desert now.

We stopped at the jumping cactus garden, a huge patch of what they called Teddybear Cholla. You can't believe what it looked like. Big cactus plants covered all over with fuzzy, cream-colored "fur" on hundreds of fat little branches that stuck out from one another in every direction. "Joints," Jay-Rod called them.

We followed the trail that wandered through the wild garden. Wouldn't ya know it, I just couldn't keep myself from reaching out carefully and trying to pet the soft-looking teddybears. Yikes! The end of one jumped off and grabbed me! Oww! It was full of microscopic (said J-R) spines that clung to my fingers.

"Don't try to pull it away with your other hand, Bro!" warned Jay-Rod.

Too late. Now I was stuck on the joint with both my hands like a fly on flypaper. Jay-Rod opened one of the guidebooks like a clam and used it to pull the cactus joint carefully off my fingers without touching the joint himself. But those invisible barbs—they were left behind—embedded! You know it!

I hear them using this word "embedded" for everything these days, from soldiers in battle zones to newspapers in garbage cans! Don't let them fool you! There is only one real meaning for "embedded." It is what a Teddybear Cholla does to your fingers when you try to pet it! Microscopic? Bikoscopic! Seeing wasn't what that cactus was about at all. Try feeling! Then you'll know all you'll ever want to know about Teddybear Cactus spines. All I wanted was for them to go back to bed, and sleep tight!

How do you get them out? Slowly. Painfully. Probably never. I still feel them when things go bad, like old men whose war wounds tell them when the weather's going to change. Jay-Rod got the worst of them out with tweezers. But I carried some of those invisible torturers in my fingers for days, let me tell you.

Mom put salve on my fingers to soften them up. And I even tried soaking them in medicinal brandy when she wasn't looking. Maybe they would dissolve like the stitches do in an operation. But I didn't dare lick the brandy off my fingers like I planned, in case they stuck onto my tongue, too!

Anything I touched with my fingers hurt like a zillion stinging bees. But I said to myself, this is not going to stop me from driving. I am a mighty spiritual being trapped inside a human body! Only the body has feeling, not the being, so I am not going to feel the pain from those embedded bee stings!

"I'm okay, Mom," I gagged, grabbing hold of Jay-Rod. "See, I can even pick up Jay-Rod. (I really hoped a few spines would embed themselves into him, but don't tell Mom)."Quit wiggling!" I hissed in his ear. "You're making it worse!"

I guess I pulled off that little stunt, because Mom let me continue driving. But sometimes I had to secretly wipe off a tear or two that would dribble down my face when the pain got too bad. Mighty spiritual beings do not cry, I tried to convince myself.

So, did we stop at the next Sonoran Desert attraction to look at the weirdo ocotillo patch? Not us. We read in the guide book that those wiry whips grow in bunches up to 20 feet in height from a single spot in the ground. But they too were covered with tiny green leaves that camouflaged barbs on their branches.

The only plant we could not help but notice were the creosote bushes stretched out in even spaces across the entire desert floor as far as the eye could see. They looked like they had been planted. Nope. These plants send out a deadly chemical from their roots to kill off any other kind of plant that tries to grow near them. They need a wide space around themselves to soak up every bit of the little rain that falls. It's every plant for itself out there on that brutal desert. We could smell the creosote. That desert seemed to stink like a freshly tarred road.

We drove all the way across it to Cottonwood Visitor's Center at the south entrance to the park. But then we saw the black SUV parked among the cars in the parking lot. It had that same license number. So I turned around quickly and headed back. All the while I felt a sort of depressing feeling, and not because of my fingers. It just wasn't the upbeat feeling of the Mohave and its rocks and Joshua Trees.

I told Jay-Rod the black SUV belongs here among the other negative residents and not back up where we were headed. He replied that the SUV sure didn't agree, since it was coming back our way now, if I cared to look around. No! It couldn't be following us again, could it? Was it after our rock again? What's going on here?

I wished out loud that our vintage bus had the power they had to climb out of this "doleful" (Jay's word) desert like that SUV was doing. Would they catch up with us? I concentrated in driving as fast as our old bus would go up the rise into the mountain pass in the distance. I didn't look either right or left, but kept my eyes glued to the road with the tips of my fingers fanning the air as I handled the wheel with the palms of my hands. Ouch!

Then suddenly we were out of it. Where was the ocotillo patch? Had we come to it yet? Where was that devilish cactus garden? Did we pass it already? Jay-Rod figured it had taken us about 30 minutes to drive down to Cottonwood. But now only 15 minutes had passed for us to get all the way back to our campground in the Mohave. And where was the black SUV? Nowhere in sight.

How did it happen? We must have lost time. If you know about UFOs, you've probably heard about cases of "missing time" by people who see UFOs when they're driving along. They suddenly find themselves home and don't remember getting there. That was us. I kid you not.

Did our rock energy do it, I wondered aloud? Jay-Rod didn't know. It was as good a theory as any. And he seemed as happy as a cactus wren, hopping around our new campground, picking up rocks, and throwing them into the air, while chanting: *Come one, come all, this rock shall fly, from its firm base, as soon as I!*

He was quoting something or other from something or other, I guess. Still our Mohave rocks were not flying. They were not even rocking any more. But they were smiling!

7

Lost

"Now, where is that boy?" That's Mom speaking. I'd heard that question a zillion times, I bet, growing up with that unpredictable kid, Jarod. He was always scampering off here and there. It did not surprise me one bit that he would go exploring among the boulders and forget to come back when he was supposed to.

"Try his cell phone," I told Mom.

But she already had. Either he had forgotten to turn it on. (No doubt). Or he didn't have it with him in the first place. (No double-doubt).

She wanted me to go look for him and not get lost myself. Okay. I showed her my turned-on cell phone and she was satisfied. No use yelling his name, I remembered from my first experience among the rocks. Sound doesn't carry when you're down among them.

Instead, I carried a canteen of water and also wore my backpack filled with dates, raisins, beef jerky, and peanut butter sandwiches enough for two, my Swiss army knife, flashlight, matches, a trail map, sun block, a sweater, a poncho (for sun not rain), and a compass. How's that? Here I come, Jay-Rod, ready or not!

The trail leading out of Hidden Valley Campground was a short, easy one. But knowing that Jay-Rod never stayed on trails, I needed everything I could cram into that backpack. So off I went.

One thing about Jay-Rod, he had no fear of anything. He could tune right in wherever he was and find out all kinds of things about the people, animals, plants, and places he visited. Also wild animals, snakes, and even wild people held no fear for him. In fact, they left him strictly alone—like he was under some kind of protection. He said he was: God's. Okay. That comes from being a mighty spiritual being, I guess. So, does that protection rub off on me too, if I am one of them? Hmm.

Okay. Now, which way should I go? I decided to take the regular Hidden Valley Nature Trail and branch off from that into the Wonderland of Rocks. Although it looks like a solid wall of rock, it isn't. Narrow valleys and desert washes "penetrate its depths," as Mom read to us. There is no official trail into its center either, just paths that climbers have made and animal trails.

Well, off I went. The trail led to a narrow gap between the rocks, opening into Hidden Valley. Where would Jay-Rod be? At first I tried closing my eyes and concentrating on him. I could see his laughing face, but that didn't tell me anything except that this was all a big joke. Some joke.

Well, maybe I could spot an animal that would lead me on. Yes. There was a big jackrabbit with its long ears, as orange inside as our bus was outside. As it bounded away I gave chase, but soon found that it was not going my way, but dodging this way and that and then circling back. It also made surprising leaps to see where I was, and then would take off in the opposite direction. Okay.

I would try following my map. That showed the Wonderland to be mostly over on the opposite side of the park road, so I headed in that direction. Problem was, you couldn't go straight anywhere. There would be some humungous boulder cutting you off with no way around it. You had to backtrack. By the time you got around that rock, you couldn't find the original wash you were following, anyway. As Jay-Rod would say: "Is a puzzlement!" So I just let myself wander through the Wonderland, this way and that—like a jackrabbit.

I knew that Jay-Rod would not plow straight ahead, anyway, but stop to look at some bug or a bird or maybe chase one of those funny little ground squirrels. They were everywhere. No roadrunners today. The shaman's bird had disappeared completely. Same with the coyote. And I was not quick enough for the ground squirrels.

Oops! I almost stumbled into a large prickly pear cactus! Wouldn't that be a hoot! Covered from head to toe with cactus spines! I could go on exhibit as The Human Pincushion! A cactus wren came out from its tangled interior to scold me. How come the spines don't hurt it?

My cell phone rang. It was Mom, of course, wondering where I was and if I was having any luck finding Jay-Rod. That call jogged my mind to try Jay's cell again, but of course, no answer.

Walking was easy over the flat ground, but I was soon swallowed up by the rocks again. There were gullies and washes here and there that looked like they might lead to some cool places. But when I tried to follow a wash it always ended up full of boulders that had to be climbed to proceed any further.

Well, I could always try meditating like I did when I got lost over at Jumbo Rocks Campground when we first arrived. I took a deep breath, closed my eyes, and tried to picture Jay-Rod. When his face came into my mind's eye I sent him a mental message:

"Jay-Rod, where are you? Mom is really worried. She sent me out to look for you. You need to come back to the camp right away. Can you find your way?"

I continued my search without getting any reply from my brother. I would stop, close my eyes, clear my mind, and listen. Nothing. Finally, my cell rang again. This time it was Jay-Rod. He had made his way back to camp, (wouldn't ya know it?) and was calling me to come back, too.

Okay. But that was the problem. I had no idea which way to go. I turned around and started back the way I thought I came, but nothing looked familiar. I had the sinking feeling that now it was me who was lost! Terrific! Talking to Jay-Rod and Mom on the phone didn't help. My description of where I was didn't mean a thing to them.

Darrell

We had no good reference points except for the sun and I couldn't tell exactly which way it was moving. I guess I could have made a sundial with a stick stuck in the ground and waited around to see which way its shadow would fall. But that took too long. What about my compass? I dug through everything in my pack and never found it! Uuh!

"If you go west a long ways you will eventually come to the park road," was Jay-Rod's less than comforting suggestion. "But there's a lot of rocks and boulders in between."

No. Too much climbing. Maybe if I lit a signal fire, the park rangers would see the smoke and come after me. Probably not. I was embedded too deep in this gigantic rock pile! Terrific! "I just wish I had a trail of crumbs to follow back to camp, like Hansel and Gretel!" I moaned aloud.

No sooner were those words spoken then, splat! A bird dropping landed on the rock where I sat! What? It was the cactus wren that had scolded me earlier. Now it was dancing around impatiently, but looking me in the eye as if to say? "Will I do? C'mon, let's go."

You're not going to believe this, (all right, you might), but I actually followed that wacky bird, and it led me straight (well almost) back to the campground! I mean, come on, who in their right mind would believe such a thing?

Jay-Rod did. He kept saying over and over: "That's your second wish."

What? You know. He reminded me that I asked to be granted three wishes for our help in healing the rocks. Wish number one was when I asked for our bus to have the power to climb out of that "doleful" Pinto Basin desert before the SUV caught us. And it happened. So now this was my second wish: to have a trail like Hansel and Gretel to follow back to the camp. And it happened. I guess that meant I had one more wish left.

That really shook me up when I thought seriously about it. Could that really have happened? Jay-Rod thought so. "Be careful, Bro, when you say your next wish out loud, 'cause it might come true." I was going to make up some crazy wish about him, but he jumped up and covered my mouth first. Yes. I would have to think about this carefully.

Mom said she needed to go back into town that afternoon to get a few supplies. Our water tank was low and so was our bus gas. "Town" around here meant Twenty-Nine Palms. A cool town: mostly one or two long streets and all the stores with murals painted on their outside walls showing scenes from the town's history.

I told Mom we ought to settle there, so she could paint murals on buildings. There were still some vacant ones left for her: the waste disposal center, for instance. She said she had already signed me up for that one. We have a lot of fun in our family, as you can see.

Did we want to go along, she asked? I really did, but Jay-Rod kept poking me and shaking his head "no." He must have something else up his fuzzy red mop, I figured. So I said "no" too. Of course she made us promise to stay around the campground, and not get lost. We could explore the rocks here. There were certainly plenty of them to crawl up and slide down on. Uh-huh.

"Now what did you have in mind, Bro?" I asked as soon as Mom was out of sight. He gave the follow-me hand signal. I picked up my backpack, and off we went. I could see we were headed out into the Wonderland of Rocks again, just where Mom probably didn't want us to go. But now I trusted that Jay knew the way, since he got back easy enough.

"I found another cave, Bro, and it has some really cool petroglyphs in it. We'll need your flashlight and something to draw with.

To get to this cave really took some doing. We had to squeeze through rock passages made for midgets, it seemed to me. Then up and over and around all kinds of boulders and obstructions. Jay thought nobody had ever found this site since the original shaman left. In fact, the tiny entrance looked like it had been sealed by a rock that finally got shoved aside—maybe by an earthquake.

Jay-Rod stopped me from trying to squeeze through the hole-like entrance until he had asked permission to enter and sprinkled a little cornmeal in front of it. He said tobacco was a better offering but he was all out of it at the moment. Inside was a forked stick standing in front of an Indian pottery bowl—an "olla"—and petroglyphs all over the back wall and ceiling. The cave had a musty animal-like smell to it.

These petroglyphs were a lot like the first ones we saw except there were no figures of people. Jay-Rod thought that meant the cave was used only for the shaman and his business. He wasn't using it for curing people. What we made out were mostly geometric figures. The ones that stood out the best were the crosses. They were either a simple plus cross (+), or a plus with an outline around it—or sometimes a double outline. Jay said those represented the Morning Star (Venus). The one I liked the best was one of the outlined crosses with a heart figure on a box at the bottom of the cross.

This cave seemed dead compared to the other one. Also the petroglyphs in this cave weren't talking to us at all. When we lightly touched the ones we could reach, we got: nothing. Jay said for me to say out loud what I thought each figure might be, and if I got a "rush" (skin prickles), what I said might be true.

Jay felt that the shaman went into his trances here at night—sort of a vision quest. When he woke up he would peck out a petroglyph to represent his journey out-of-body, or what he had seen while he was "astral-traveling." We both got rushes on that. I said I felt that the outlined cross with the heart and box at the bottom meant that the shaman had traveled out-of-body to Venus, the planet of love. I got a rush on that.

It was strange what I got about the heart. I really felt that it represented Earth—that the shaman was supposed to bring back love to Earth. (Maybe he carried it in the petroglyph box!) I got a rush on that, too.

Now we both felt a definite drop in temperature. I knew what that meant: some kind of energy was present. It didn't feel friendly at all. "Let's get out of here, Bro," whispered Jay-Rod abruptly. "Don't touch the stick or the olla. They're protected." We both scrambled back through the little entrance hole and started running..

"Hoo-boy! What was that?" I let out when we finally had run as far as we could before collapsing. Jay-Rod said many shamans were powerful figures that you didn't mess around with. He didn't know if that cold energy represented a shaman or not. But we were really trespassing on private property without permission, and the owner didn't like it. I reminded him he had asked for permission when he sprinkled the cornmeal.

"Yeah, but I didn't hear anybody give it to us."

"Well, what could a shaman do to us, anyway? Aren't we supposed to be mighty spiritual beings?"

"Darry, Darry," replied Jay-Rod in his talking-to-a-kindergartner voice. "First of all, we have to protect ourselves. You do that by visualizing a golden light of protection all around you. Then you must state your intent: that you are doing this in order to help others, and not for yourself. Did you do that?"

"Of course, not. Did you?" I guess I had a lot to learn about shamans, invisible beings, friendly and unfriendly energy, and all. I guess I had a lot to learn about being a mighty spiritual being. It was not like putting on a Superman suit and flying out to sock the bad guys. Kapow! How did Jay know all this without even cracking a book?

"I was born knowing some things, ol' Buddy. And I had to go to school to learn the rest," he replied.

"School? What school? No school I ever heard of teaches you how to see invisible things and talk to animals."

"Mine does. And so does yours. We go to school at night when we're asleep to learn spiritual things. But I remember in the daytime what I've learned at night, and you don't. You're not supposed to—yet. But you will. When things change on Earth, then you'll suddenly wake up one day with all sorts of knowledge and abilities. Be patient, my teachers tell me."

"Your teachers? Who are they?" I wanted to know.

"Well, they're sort of like—angels."

Knock me over with a feather! That's the second time Jay-Rod ever told me anything about his special abilities. And I will get them too? From angels? Cool!

All this time we were sitting at the base of a boulder where we had collapsed from running away from the cave. Now we definitely heard some rumbling from back where the cave was located. Time to be on our way again. This was not the time to wait around to find out what was causing that noise.

Back at the campsite Mom was really upset. But not with us. She hardly noticed we'd been gone. No. Something else had happened while she was out on her run to town for supplies. On the way back she stopped at the Visitors Center for a book to read, got back in the bus, and as she was driving along she realized one of her rings was missing off her finger. Gone. Her most precious Zuni ring that Dad had given her. She never took it off. How could it be missing? She held up her hand to show us. Where could it be? She looked ready to cry.

Jay-Rod said we'd help her find it tomorrow. It was too late to go back there tonight. I said we were mighty spiritual beings and we had powers. We'd find the ring for her. Jay-Rod gave me a poke in the ribs with his elbow and a scowl. So much for the day of the losts.

8

The Zuni Ring

"Think, think, think, Mom! When did you first notice it was missing?" That was Jarod giving Mom the "third degree" (whatever that is) about her missing ring. Everybody turned to Jarod to help them find the things they lost. He could do it, too. He would put them through this series of questions and make them think back till they came up with an answer. That usually gave them the clue they needed to find the object themselves.

He said that most people really knew where they mislaid their missing objects, but their brains somehow blocked this information. He was a brain-unlocker, he said. More like a "drain-unstopper," was my reply. (We had this thing with words.)

Anyway, he had Mom visualize the ring in all its detail, just like it was still on her finger—and that ring had plenty of detail that all of us knew about. It was an unusual square-face ring made by a Zuni Indian silversmith, who inlaid it in 13 triangles with four different stones: mother-of-pearl, turquoise, coral, and obsidian.

It was set in a fancy silver setting with four tiny obsidian circles, one for each of the four directions. Around the outside of the silver band were engraved or stamped arrows, circles, half-moons, and two eight-pointed stars. On the inside near the jeweler's mark were two little figures that looked like running petroglyph figures. As I said—plenty of detail!

I think we loved that ring as much as Mom did. Dad bought it for her when they were out on one of their summer petroglyph hunts in New Mexico. They visited the Zuni reservation and admired the inlaid work the jewelers did. I know you're going to ask if a Zuni silversmith actually made it for her. No. Although I think she wished one did. They weren't anywhere near

Zuni when they found the ring in a trading post store in Arizona. Mom said it was "old pawn." In case you think that's not good, think again.

Old pawn is some of the finest Indian jewelry around, she said. It's jewelry made by some of the best of the old silversmiths with some of the best old silver and precious stones. Sometimes when Indians had a need for cash they would take their jewelry to a trading post or pawn shop and pawn it for money.

If they never came back to claim their jewelry it would be put in the "old pawn" display cabinet and sold. Mom felt she was very lucky to find such a wonderful ring. And now it was gone.

I felt bad about it too. Jarod and me used to make up stories about the Indian who made it and what the different symbols stood for. The arrows were sometimes for battles he won, or sometimes for hunting buffalo. (Did the Zunis hunt buffalo?) Never mind.

I loved to make up stories about the suns, moons, and stars on it. Jay-Rod said Native Americans believe their ancestors came from the stars. Cool. My Indian practiced magic and could travel to the moon. Jarod would sometimes pretend to be one of the little figures beating me in a race. Mom would let us look at it and even take it off for us, but she never let us handle it for long. Too precious, she always said. And now it was gone.

I felt bad because I thought she would have a hard time getting it back. Anyone who found that ring would probably want to keep it. Most people aren't that honest when it comes to valuable things, is my opinion.

But I knew Jay-Rod would give it his best finder's try. After all, he was the one who said this was a traveler's ring. He meant *really* going places. He said the lines of the triangle inlays on the surface of the ring made a star map, like the Nazca lines on the desert in Peru. (Where does he get this stuff?) He said the captain of a UFO could use the ring to find his way back home to a different gallaxy! Wow! And now it was gone.

Why didn't I use my third wish to try to get the ring back? As a matter of fact, I did. I made a very strong wish out loud for Mom to find her ring as soon as possible. But nothing happened. Maybe those wishes were all in our heads, after all. Jarod felt the wishes only applied to the one who made the wish. You couldn't wish for things for other people. Too bad.

"Well, when did you first notice her ring was missing?" Jarod was still pressing Mom to answer his questions.

"Oh, yes," she told him. "Now I remember. It was in the restroom at the Visitor Center. I went to wash my hands and then saw that—oh, no—the Zuni ring was gone!"

She, of course, reported it to the information desk in the Center. They quizzed her on what camp sites she had been staying at, and suggested she post a missing notice with the $50 reward. And she did. They also suggested that she look carefully in her vehicle, our orange bus. So we did. Nothing.

But Jarod kept asking her about when she last remembered having the ring on her finger. Oh, yes, she finally did remember that, too.

"I was just outside in the Visitor Center courtyard. A woman I had been talking to in the building admired it. When we walked outside, the woman asked if she could see it. Oh. Why didn't I remember that before?" she wondered.

It's sure strange the tricks your mind plays—because she had actually taken the ring off and let the woman look at it—and then forgot all about it!

"And then what happened, Mom? Think! Think! Think!"

She couldn't remember putting the ring back on! No, something else interfered. What was it? Oh, yes. A park policeman suddenly ran out of his office, jumped in his patrol car, turned on the siren, and sped away.

And then what? Well, all she could remember was getting back in the bus and driving to our campsite—and then noticing the ring was not on her finger. These new facts started a frantic search of the Visitor Center courtyard by everybody around.

Now we'll never find it, I remember thinking. Any one of those people might stumble on it and pocket it without anybody noticing. You can tell I'm some kind of a skeptic when it comes to people, can't ya?

"What d'ya think, Jay-Rod?" I wanted to know. There he stood over by the wall of the building in the shade watching everybody scrambling around, looking.

"I don't think it's here. Right here in this courtyard, I mean. I think it's around here somewhere, though. But not on the ground. Maybe off the ground about waist high." Whoa!

If it's off the ground about waist high, where would that put it? I started walking around with my arm held out about waist high like Frankenstein, listing possibilities out loud: on the bench—no, on the shelf—no, on the window ledge—no, in the trash container—? We dumped it out and went through the trash. (Yuk!) No. What about in somebody's pocket? In somebody's car? On top of that barrel cactus? Now I was getting a little too off-the-wall!

But Jay-Rod, the detective, was still not finished asking questions. "What about the woman, Mom? Did she give the ring back to you? Think. Think. Think!"

She drew a blank. That police siren had interrupted her thoughts. But now she began to think that maybe the woman had not given it back. So what did the woman look like? Well, she had dark skin, something like an Indian; black hair drawn back into a pony tail; in a tan jacket, and yes, a red skirt.

"Yes, I definitely remember the red skirt, because everyone else had on either shorts or long pants. That must be it! It must be that woman who took my ring!"

Suddenly I came up with some sort of deja-vu (or whatever you call it). Oh-man! That's what the woman from the black SUV looked like! The one who had taken Jay-Rod's picture at the Joshua Tree! I was sure of it! What's going on here?

Well, that started a whole new train of actions. Mom reported her to the park police and gave them a description. I gave them the license number of the SUV. They must have been puzzled that we knew so much about someone we didn't know. They would put out a search for her and let us know.

So back we started for camp. We hopped aboard the ol' marmalade bus, but guess what? We had a surprise passenger inside: the cactus wren! Yes, that same wren who had hopped aboard Jay-Rod's head on that first day was now fluttering around in the back. Whoa! Mom had left a window open, and you know what kind of invitation that was for such a nosy bird. What next! We finally shooed him out and went on our way.

Now that was settled, Mom thought. The park police would pick up the woman, and she would get her ring back. But Jay-Rod wasn't so sure, and that bothered me. He didn't think the woman took it.

"Well, why was she so interested in the ring, then?" Mom and me wanted to know.

He didn't know. Maybe she was more interested in Mom than the ring, was his only thought on the subject. Why would that be? He didn't know. Hmm.

We had only a week left before we'd have to pack up and go. Mom kept checking in with the Visitor Center every day, but nothing turned up. Where was the woman? Nobody seemed to know. But something kept gnawing at Jay-Rod. He still felt the ring was waist-high somewhere near the Visitor Center.

He tried meditating on it, but all he got was the ring itself embedded in green or gray or tan stuff. I said let's go back there and look around. Green or gray could be vegetation, and tan could be sand or rocks.

So we did. Maybe Mom dropped the ring in the dusty vegetation. Maybe the woman hid it under the bark of one of the trees. Maybe it's in the lady's purse and she hid that in the bushes. We got thinking up all the crazy things that could have happened to the ring—which got us laughing as we drove back there, and me sounding off again in verse , of course:

Pussy said to the owl, "You elegant fowl,
    How charmingly sweet you sing!
    Oh, let us be married too long we have tarried:
    But what shall we do for a ring? A ring?
    But what shall we do for a ring?

Of course, Jay-Rod chimed in with more of the Edward Lear verse:
    And there in a wood a piggy-wig stood,
    With a ring at the end of his nose, his nose.
    With a ring at the end of his nose.

We never did get to the end of it before we pulled into the Visitor Center, which bothered Jay-Rod, no doubt. He always liked to finish that poem in a shrill voice with the *runcible spoon* part, and then "dancing by the light of the moon" which he did. Oh, well.

Someone was waiting for us at the Visitor Center. The park police! We thought they were going to tell us they caught the woman and got the ring back. No. They found the woman, all right. But she angrily denied taking the ring. Didn't know what they were talking about. Instead, she told them that some boys in an orange bus had broken into her SUV and stolen an important rock! Yikes!

"But she took that rock from us," I tried to explain. "My brother found it, and she broke into our bus and took it when we were out hiking!"

Where was the rock now, the park ranger wanted to know? I looked at Jay-Rod and Jay-Rod looked at me. Then we both looked at the ranger with blank looks on our faces. (Well, that wasn't a lie, was it?)

I'm glad the woman wasn't there. It was her word against ours, and you know who wins an argument between kids and an adult. I told the man he could call our mom on her cell phone and she would tell him the same thing. I also got up the nerve to ask the man why the rock was so valuable. It looked like fools' gold to us.

I shouldn't have mentioned gold. That got him going. There was real gold in the mountains, and not so long ago, he told us. Had we been to any of the old mines? No. Is that where we found the rock? No. Did we know nobody was allowed to do any more gold digging in the mountains? No. Did we know we couldn't take the rock with us when we left? Yes. After a bunch of similar questions, I guess the ranger decided we were a just a couple of know-nothing kids, and let us go.

I also got the definite feeling he was not going to pursue the missing ring any further, either. Somebody was lying, and he wasn't the one to decide who. I wanted to ask him if there were any uranium mines around, but Jay-Rod turned me around quickly and pushed me out the ranger's door.

So where did that leave us? I sat down on a bench outside the Visitor Center and shook my head. The only words I could think to mutter were:

Waist high, waist high,
The ring is hiding, waist high.
Is it a lie?

That old cactus wren was back again. This time he wasn't bothering Jay-Rod who was stooping and snuffling around the outside of the building. He was after me, what d'ya know? He even hopped up on the bench beside me and started dancing around. He acted just like the cactus wren that guided me out of the Wonderland of Rocks. You know, the Hansel-and-Gretel bird. Well, maybe I should get up and follow this one.

Yes, that was it. He acted real excited when I came with him. He flapped his wings and sort of danced up and down. Where did he lead me? Uuh! Back to his nest in the middle of that big cholla cactus tangle next to the Visitor Center entrance.

I watched him disappear through the cactus branches. Then he reappeared and this time flapped over and landed on my head! Just like he did to Jay-Rod that first day!

Before I could say a thing, he flew back into the cactus again. Now Jay-Rod was watching the performance and laughing.

"He wants you to go in there, Bro! Guess he doesn't know how allergic you are to cactus spines!"

Then Jay-Rod got this bright idea. I should open all the windows of our nearby bus, go inside, and sit very still. So I did. You know what happened, don't you? The bird flew into the bus again, and this time with something shiny in its beak: the Zuni ring!!!

9

Gold Mine

Mom, of course, was overjoyed to get her ring back. When we told her the story of the cactus wren in the bus she actually believed us! Mainly because her memory began to return.

She remembered that after she was startled by the ranger's siren, she did get the ring back from the woman. Instead of putting it on, she now remembered setting it down next to her purse on the bench. She then rummaged through her purse for the car keys—which took awhile. Then she grabbed up her purse, (probably knocking the ring to the ground), went into the restroom, and discovered the ring was missing.

The cactus wren must have picked it up and put it in its nest. It could have. They're good-sized birds, you know—not little wrens like we have in Florida.

No wonder the woman was angry at being accused of stealing the ring. But we got the feeling that she didn't make the connection about the ring and us in the orange bus. Whew! She never saw Mom drive away in the bus. It was just a coincidence that the rock-stealing lady was also the one who looked at Mom's ring. "Synchronicity," said Jay-Rod.

If you don't know what that means, don't ask Jay-Rod. He'll go into a long, boring lecture on how everything we do is connected to everything everybody else does—and at certain points in time they meet. That's right. I kid you not.

We call these impossible happenings a coincidence, as if they're not real. But they are real, claims Jay. Sometimes they save us from having an accident. Sometimes they bring us together with someone we should meet. And sometimes they tell us important things like: not to take a certain plane or trip, or to stay home. That's right. Coincidences are happenings we really need to take notice of, says Jay-Rod.

Well, we already knew enough to watch out for that lady and her black SUV. But we still didn't know what to make of Jay-Rod's buzzing rock. So we decided to check out some of the old gold mines. Yeah-man!

Mom's guide book told us about them. I was all set for finding some gold. Jay-Rod told me to take it easy, that gold was not lying around on the ground for anybody to find any more. It was embedded (there's that word again!) in other minerals like quartz. It had to be separated by hard work—like being dug or blasted out of the quartz. Then it had to be crushed in stamping mills. And that was just for starters.

"Okay. Then how come you see pictures of miners with tin pans washing nuggets of gold out of streams?" I wanted to know.

He had an answer for that, too. Those pieces were "placer gold," flakes of gold that eroded away from underground veins of gold and washed down the mountains.

"You don't see any streams of water out here, do you Darry?

So what? I knew that water from rainstorms made all these washes in the first place. Maybe they also washed down some gold from some of these mountains. I mean, why did Jay-Rod think that glittering rock he found the first day was gold, I wanted to know?

He said it was the buzzing that attracted him first, not the glittering. Hmm. I decided to keep my eyes peeled for gold on the ground anyway when we hiked through washes near the old mines. Yeah-man!

Contact Mine, Desert Queen Mine, Lost Horse Mine, Eagle Cliff Mine, Eldorado, Golden Bee Mine, Johnny Lang Mine, Mastodon Mine, Ming Mine, and Silver Bell Mine. Whoa! Those were just some of the mines in the mountains around here. You can see there must have been a lot of gold. We knew we couldn't check out all of them, so how should we choose? I said make a circle of ten rocks, one for each of those mines. Then we could flip a coin above the circle and whichever rock the coin lands nearest to is the one.

Jay-Rod said no, we should check out Mom's book *On Foot in Joshua Tree National Park* and see which one we could get to without killing ourselves. They're all up high in the mountains, he said. So we checked out the book.

Our choice: Lost Horse Mine. It didn't sound too difficult. What we liked best was the story connected with it—a real wild west tale. It seems that Johnny Lang, an old prospector, lost his horse in the mountains. He followed its tracks to the cabin of cattle thief Jim McHaney.

McHaney told him his horse was no longer lost, but he better git lost himself! They all packed guns in those days, but Lang wasn't ready to use his in unfamiliar territory. Still he wasn't about to give up on the horse either.

He ended up buying a nearby gold claim from another prospector. Then he took in a couple of men as partners to help him ward off McHaney. He struck it rich in 1895 and named the claim Lost Horse Mine, for spite. It turned out to be one of the richest mines in Joshua Tree Park, producing nearly three million dollars of gold over the next ten years!

Getting the gold over to Twenty-nine Palms was almost as hard as getting it out of the ground, he found out. Too many people knew about the gold. Too many had guns they were willing to use. The gold shipments had to be disguised, and the miners had to keep armed guards around.

But then Lang himself got caught by his partners for pocketing part of the gold during his shift in the mine. They told him to sell out his stake in the mine or go to jail. He sold out. Afterward he lived in a nearby canyon for years off his stolen gold and his neighbors' cattle, so they say.

But finally one winter night when he had nothing left, he tacked a note on his door: "Gone for grub. Be back soon." He never came back. They found his remains three months later in March, 1925 where he froze to death in his canvas sleeping bag. A rough tombstone still stands on his grave where they found him. How's that for a real-life thriller?

One more thing. Right after Lang sold out, his partners struck a fault in the mine and the gold ran dry! How's that for "synchronicity"?

So we started out with high hopes for our own Lost Horse Mine adventure. I told Jay-Rod okay, as long as we don't get ourselves lost. He never had to worry about getting lost himself. But I wasn't sure there'd be any cactus wrens around to rescue me!

Most of the Joshua Trees around the mining area were long gone—used for fuel during the mining days, and I didn't see any cholla cactus either.

We parked the bus at the Lost Horse parking lot and hiked up an old abandoned wagon road most of the way. Hey, this was a piece of cactus candy! I thought the mine trails were supposed to be steep. I should have kept my mouth shut! Suddenly this one twisted so steeply up the mountain we slid one step backward for every two steps forward! It ended at the old ten-stamp mill where the gold ore was crushed.

That rusted old piece of machinery stuck out like a marmalade bus on the cleared-off mountainside. What a racket it must have made when it was going full blast. Oh-oh. It looked like there might be somebody up there. I wish we'd brought Mom's binoculars.

What was that? I swear I heard a gun shot echoing through the hills. It was a sharp crack of some kind. Guess I was jumpy because of all the other strange happenings. I was always alert for the lady from the black SUV—especially since the park police said she accused us of stealing Jay-Rod's rock. Sounds just like a modern wild west story, doesn't it?

There it went again! Cr-rack! Jay-Rod looked in that direction too, but didn't seemed disturbed by it. Hey, there was somebody up there! I definitely saw a person darting in and out of the bushes along a ridge.

"Hey, Jay-Rod, whatd'ya think? You don't suppose they still have guards stationed around an abandoned mine, do you?"

"Well, let's get up there and find out! Whoopee!" he shouted, and started galloping up the trail.

Totally fearless. That was Jay-Rod. The only thing he said to watch out for were rattlesnakes under bushes—and vertical mine shafts. You know, the holes in the ground that go straight down for maybe a hundred feet. Stay away from them, he cautioned, 'cause they might cave in and down you would go—swoosh! Never to be seen again forevermore. He liked to be dramatic.

The mine entrance and shafts around the Lost Horse Mine were all sealed with grating, so there wasn't anything dangerous about them. We scrambled up some wooden stairs to the next level. Some rusty old tanks turned out to be cyanide settling tanks. They were used for separating gold from the crushed ore. Uuh! Pretty poisonous it sounded to me! Stone building foundations and other rusted-out mining equipment were scattered around. A really steep trail took us up to the top of the mountain.

We were huffing and puffing with our eyes on the trail when suddenly this gruff voice growled out: "Hey, you kids, whatdya think yer doin' up here? Lose yer way or sumpthin'?" There was an old man sitting on a rock with a rifle in one hand and a burlap sack in the other.

"No, sir," Jay-Rod spoke right up. "We were just looking at the old mine. That's all. Guess there's no more gold around here these days." That's Jay-Rod, always friendly and polite no matter who he's speaking to.

"Gold? Yer after gold? Well, you sure come to the wrong place. There's no gold on this here mountain. Why d'ya think I'd be here huntin' rabbits if there was any gold around? Only fools look for gold around here. And yer only kids. Not fools yet, I guess."

"What about placer gold?" I cut in.

"Placer gold? Well, there's sure none of that on top of this here mountain or any other one I knowed of. If yer lookin' for placer gold, which is long gone, yer really off yer track. Only placer gold around here is—er was, over t' Dale. Ya know where that is? Of course, ya don't. It's gone. Ya take the Old Dale Road over in the Pinto Basin and drive till ya can't drive no more."

All of a sudden I heard a low sort of rumbling noise. What was that? It almost seemed like the ground beneath our feet was moving—trembling a little. A few rocks rolled down from up above and went bouncing on down the mountainside, raising dust as they went. Then it stopped.

The old guy laughed. "Just a little earthquake. A baby one. They call 'em tremlers. Now if they was a real quake like we had back in the '60's, we'd all go a-slidin' down this here mountain, just like them rocks. Whatcha lookin' so scared for? Didn't ya know we was settin' on top of some of the biggest Earth cracks on this here planet?

"Why that there San Andreas Fault that nearly wrecked San Francisco is lyin' just south of this here park. And north of here is the Pinto Basin Fault. Yessiree, these here mountains was all pushed up the way they is today by them faults. An' I hear-tell we got another big quake comin.' That'll bring up the gold from down below, er else bury it deeper 'n Death Valley. Yessiree."

At this he reached in his sack, pulled out an old canteen and took a healthy swig of whatever was in it. Both Jay-Rod and I decided without saying a word it was time to take our leave, so we did. We scrambled and slid back down the mountainside to the mine ruins. Then we beat a rocky retreat on down the old wagon road and back to our bus without looking back.

"Who was that?"

I couldn't hold it in any longer. Was he a real person, hunting in a national park? Talking like an old prospector? Dressed like one too. Or some kind of ghost? Jay-Rod just shook his head. People do have flashbacks and things like déjà vu. You know—where they seem to be in scenes from another time period. But we both witnessed the same person and heard the same words, so he must have been real. And what did he mean about another big earthquake? Both of us also felt the Earth tremor. Was the San Andreas Fault really so close?

Never mind the earthquake. You know what we did next? Found out where the Old Dale Road was and headed out! It was down in that weird Pinto Basin where we had our lost time experience, wouldn't ya know it?

One of Mom's guide books told about the boomtown of Dale springing up in the 1880's when placer gold was discovered in the washes, and then in mines all through the mountains. The town had a population of over a thousand in the early 1880s. It had a store, a post office, a blacksmith shop, an assay office, and a saloon. Most of the miners lived in framed tents they could move when one mine gave out and another was discovered.

So Dale was a sort of movable town. It went where the gold was. When the gold gave out so did Dale. Today there is nothing left but abandoned mines, and open vertical shafts. Uuh!

Jay-Rod was concerned about me driving across that basin on the Old Dale Road. A sign at the turn-off warned: "Road Not Maintained. 4 Wheel Drive Vehicles Only." I told Jay I would turn back if the road became too bumpy and impassable. Well, we made it over to the mountains. After that it got pretty bad, so we parked and walked in. We saw some of the old mine openings up in the hills, but we stayed pretty close to the washes.

Jarod

Jay-Rod picked up some interesting pieces of fool's gold, but none of them buzzed, he said. I brought along a frying pan and sifter out of the bus for the placer mining I planned on doing. How can you sift gold out of sand and gravel without water, he wanted to know? Watch me!

I scooped up some likely looking dirt with the frying pan. Then I picked out the larger pieces of gravel with my fingers. I could even sift much of it out with one of Mom's flour sifters. (Don't tell Mom!). But then there was all that sand and dust at the bottom. I tried blowing it off. That worked but it got up my nose. Then I tried fanning it off with my hat and that worked even better. When it finally got down to the very bottom I pour a little water from my canteen into the pan and sloshed it around. Then I poured the remains through a white dish towel from the bus. Hey, I was getting pretty good at this! Finally one of my pannings seemed to show something yellow!

Jay-Rod! Take a look at this! Doesn't that yellow stuff look like gold to you? He looked, and looked some more. Then he looked up at me. "Darrell," he said, "I think you've struck it rich!" Was he kidding? Maybe not. I put the tiny flakes in the plastic jar I brought along, and went back to my panning for gold.

When it was finally time to pack up and turn back, I had a tidy little cache (of gold?). Jay-Rod had a back-ache from stooping over, looking for buzzing rocks and such stuff. You know what happens to me when I'm happy? Right! I sing! Or chant.

So as we barreled back up the Pinto Basin highway, I was hollering out the open window:

Behold! Behold!
   We found us some gold!
   Who could have foretold
   We'd find us some gold?

Jay-Rod said I was as dumb as all the other prospectors who broadcast their findings so loud everybody rushes to get some, and soon it's all gone. Anyway, he said mine was nothing but dust.

Mom was happy we made it back safely from our latest expedition. I was still in a singing mood. But when I broke into my latest rendition of *"What Can We Do For a Battered Boulder?"* she stopped me, saying there was something more important we could do for our orange bus right now. Get out the lug wrench and car jack. We had a flat tire! Uuh! Now where did that come from?

10

Oasis of Mara

Mom planned to go out of the park for the morning to Twenty-nine Palms to get supplies and drop off the flat tire to get it fixed. She said she would drop us off at any place we chose between our camp and the Visitor Center. Then she would pick us up at noon on her way back. We could still keep in touch with our cell phones. So where did we want to be dropped off?

We both knew where. Jay-Rod had seen it in a dream. I just knew where from a feeling I had: the Oasis of Mara behind the Visitor Center. But there was one more thing. We needed a really big favor from Mom. Jay-Rod decided he should be the one to ask, since she usually took him more serious than me.

"Mom, we have a tremendous favor to ask of you. It is very *imperative* for us to borrow your Zuni ring for a few hours. Just while you're gone to town. Don't worry. We'll guard it with our lives."

Well, Mom did take Jay seriously, but she was still uncertain. Look what happened when she took off the ring before. Yes, we understood that. But this time Jay would wear it on a chain around his neck under his shirt. Nobody would see it, and how could he lose it? How could she refuse when he said "imperative"? That meant vital, essential, and crucial all rolled up into one. After all, he was the one who pointed out the star map on the surface of the ring.

Yes. She got the point. But why did we want it in the first place, she wanted to know? If we told her the truth that Jay-Rod saw it in a dream; that he was wearing the ring at the Oasis, what would she say? In the end he said he wanted to make a wish with the ring at the Oasis spring.

That was sort of the truth. Or at least close enough. We didn't really know why he should wear the ring at the Oasis. Making a wish seemed like a safe reason. Mom knew that Jay-Rod often had weird reasons for doing things, so... Okay. She finally agreed. Jay high-fived me and did a dance around the bus. Mom put the ring on one of her jewelry chains and hung it around Jay-Rod's neck. Then she dropped us off at the Visitor Center and took off for town.

We could see the Oasis just down a paved path in back of the Center. Tall California fan palm trees with their thick brown "skirts" of thatch were clumped together in the middle of the Oasis. They were packed in close by other desert bushes. Then on down the path were more palms growing separately. Used to be called Twenty-nine Palms Oasis, said the guide book. That's where the town got its name from.

You probably know that a desert oasis comes from permanent water at the surface—sometimes a pool, sometimes a spring—where trees grow. There's no water anywhere else in a true desert, we learned, except for sudden downpours that end as quickly as they start. Their water may gush down washes in flash floods, but finally it sinks into the ground and disappears.

In the beginning underground water at the Oasis of Mara was forced up into springs by the Pinto Mountain fault nearby. But these days the water table is too low for springs. Water has to be piped in by the Park Service to keep the trees from dying. Too bad. We've really interfered with nature even in a National Park, I noted sadly. Jay-Rod corrected me on that one, saying that our country saved the trees by making the park in the first place.

But he didn't stay around long enough to say much of anything else. First he gave the biggest palm tree back of the Visitor Center a partial hug. It was so big around that it would take three Jay-Rods to hug it completely! Then off he went charging down the half-mile-long trail that circled the Oasis, running, skipping, and even doing a cartwheel of sorts.

Good thing we got here before the tourists, I noted, or somebody would have slowed him down for sure. Around he went whipping past mesquite bushes, prickly pear cactus, yucca, desert-willow, cottonwood, saltbush, and of course the palm trees. When he reappeared on the far side of the Oasis he was twirling as he went, arms straight out like a helicopter ready to take-off.

"Hey, Bro, slow down! The trees want to talk to you, but they can't even get a word in edgewise!"

"I'm doing the palm-tree polka, Darry-boy! The trees are so happy we're here they want to yank up their roots and dance for joy! So I'm doing it for them!" And round he went again.

What are you gonna to do with a kid like that? He was probably already communicating with the trees through osmosis, (whatever that is). When he finally came to a halt, he flopped down exhausted on the bench next to me. Now what happens, I wondered?

"What's our next move, oh Mighty Spiritual Being?"

"You know, Darry, you sound like none of this is serious or important. Like you don't remember what the boulders at Jumbo Rocks said about this being a sacred place; about how they needed help; or how the shaman told us we were chosen to help heal the rocks and trees and all. And did you forget the rock energy that went inside us and is still there? C'mon, Bro, get with the program."

"Yeah-man, I remember. I remember. It's just that someone in this weirdo family needs to play it straight. Needs to keep us on track. That's all. So I was just wondering, what's next?"

"What's next is meditating. You sit here on the bench and try it. I'm going into the middle of the Oasis where the spring is, and try it. Then we can compare notes. I think we really should get something important. Remember, the shaman at the first cave told us to visit Mara; and this is Mara."

Hoo-boy! I was still pretty jumpy about all this. Okay, I would try meditating, but I didn't know if I really wanted to get anything or not. The whole idea of it was still pretty nerve-rattling to me.

Finally I closed my eyes and tried to blank out my mind. All I could see was purple, not red like at the Heart Rock. Hmm. Then nothing. Then just before I gave up and got ready to open my eyes, I felt—but didn't hear—a thought. The thought was that I should stand up and look over toward the town of Twenty-nine Palms. So I did. I walked across the path and stood next to a historical marker overlooking the desert in that direction.

I could easily see across the small expanse of desert over to the highway, to the town, and to the mountains beyond. Between the park and the highway I saw a long stretch of ground raised up in a line parallel to the highway. It stretched as far as I could see with brush growing on it—like someone had dug a long ditch and left the dirt piled up.

The historical marker said that line marked the Pinto Mountain Fault. Whoa! It ran east-west along the north boundary of the park. The line was called a "scarp." It was the raised up edge of an underground fault (crack) in the Earth. Oh-wow! The land on one side of the scarp was higher than the land on the other side. That was where the Earth had cracked open and moved during an earthquake. Uuuh! Did I really want to know about this? The marker also said that magnitude-7 earthquakes had occurred along this fault in 1992 and 1999. Hoo-boy! That really brought me back to life in a hurry. Is that what I was supposed to look at? Was my "thought" a warning that another earthquake was due?

When I turned to sit back down on my bench, I saw it was already taken by an older man all in white: shoes, pants, shirt, and hair. He even had a white carnation in his buttonhole. And now that I noticed it, he was wearing a white tie! Whoa! Why was he dressed so formally for a hike in the desert? Maybe he was on his way to a wedding or something. He grinned at me when he saw me gawking, and moved over so I had room to sit.

"Did I take your seat, young fellow? Sorry. I saw you get up and thought you had vacated the bench for good. My mistake. You were reading that historical marker, I noticed. Tells all about the Earth movements around here, doesn't it? Pretty impressive to think that this park is sitting on top of some of the most active faults in the entire continent. What do you think about that?"

He really caught me off guard, and for a change I was speechless. I was still trying to digest what I had just read. It almost seemed like he picked up on my "thought."

"Well, that's all right," he said, getting up, lighting up a cigar, and starting off on his way down the path. "We all have to go someday in someway, so I wouldn't worry about it."

At that moment Jay-Rod rushed up. I tried to get him to look at the departing man, but when we turned, the man was gone. That path was half a mile long in plain sight and he was nowhere on it, nor out on the desert, nor in the Oasis. So what happened to him?

What Jay-Rod had to tell me sent my thoughts spinning off in another direction, and I soon forgot about the man. He said this Oasis was the site for a Serrano Indian village for hundreds of years. They were finally driven out by disease and destruction by white settlers in the late 1800s and early 1900s. He said when he closed his eyes their whole history paraded before him like a slide show.

All he had to do was ask how they lived on the desert and he would see them hunting rabbits with throwing-sticks that looked like boomerangs; or picking fruits from the prickly pear cactus with sticks; or grinding mesquite pods for flour; or roasting and eating the Joshua Tree flowers; or making pottery *ollas* to store water and food; or placing forked "spirit sticks" in caves to protect the ollas inside. Whoa!

His invisible slide show also showed them weaving palm and yucca fibers into hats, sandals, baskets, nets, and rope. Then they were building round thatched houses with a central fire pit; and sharing food and water with the first prospectors who came looking for gold. In the end they were dying from smallpox brought in by the early settlers; or being burned out by unruly white gangs; and being forced to leave by the railroad that claimed to own the land. At the same time they practiced powerful ceremonies at the central spring in the Oasis. But finally the deva of the spring left the Oasis, and the people felt the presence of evil spirits, so they left too.

Jay-Rod could go on for hours, it seemed, about the lives of those Indians from the scenes he saw while he meditated at the spring. It's like his mind sucked in great thought-bundles as the scenes crossed his mind's eye. He thought Mom's ring had something to do with this Indian "slide show."

But what does it all mean for us, I wanted to know? He couldn't tell me. He was so wrapped up in the story of the Indians, he couldn't seem to think about anything else.

I could understand that. Here was a group of people who had made their homes in this beautiful, peaceful desert without harming anybody. Then the white man moved in and wrecked it all.

Where are they now, I wondered? Are there any Serranos left? Jay-Rod knew that, too. All those who were left finally moved over to the Morongo Reservation in Banning, California years ago.

"C'mon, Jay-Rod," I pleaded, "think about what this means for us. What is this *deva* you talked about? And what about the evil spirits?" That seemed to stir him a bit, and he looked around.

"A deva is a nature spirit, Bro," he finally came out with. "The deva of this Oasis was the great protector of the place," he said. "Once she was gone, other negative spirits could come in."

Suddenly I got her name. It was *Marrah*, not Mara as it is spelled today. The guide books say "mara" was a Serrano word meaning "place of little springs and much grass." But I got it was also the name of the deva. "Marrah," I said it aloud.

As we looked back toward the center of the Oasis, a light mist seemed to be radiating out from it. Jay-Rod started jumping up and down and pointing. "There she is! The deva! See her, Darry! There's Marrah! She's back!"

Well, I have to admit I didn't see anything but the mist. That was surprising enough, I guess. You don't see mists around the desert in the middle of the day. Tourists were now beginning to walk down the path toward the Oasis, and I could see they were curious about Jay-Rod's excitement.

I said to one lady, "He's just excited about seeing the mist over the Oasis." The lady looked up and shook her head. "What mist?" she replied. "I don't see any mist."

Wouldn't ya know it? What could I say?

Now I noticed that one of the tourists was none other than Mom, back from her trip to town. She wanted to know if we were ready to go back to the camp. Jay-Rod shook his head, no. I could tell he had other things in mind for us to do at the Oasis, so I said I would take Mom back and drive the bus back here.

No, Jarod would have to come too, according to Mom, and then I could drive the two of us back. She felt it wasn't a great idea to leave a ten-year-old boy behind by himself. Especially ours.

So off we went again. By the time we got back in the early afternoon the tourists had cleared out and the mist was gone. Jay-Rod said we both needed to go into the middle of the Oasis where he had been and sit on the rocks there to meditate. Again he sprinkled some cornmeal around and asked the deva for permission. I wondered if I would get an Indian slide show in my head like Jay-Rod's. No luck. Oh, well, I wasn't the one with the ring.

Instead I heard a distinct voice in my head as I meditated. It said: "This is the place, young fellow, where it's all going to start. The Earth changes, you know. But you have performed a wonderful deed by healing the Heart Rock and spreading its energy across the park.

"You have released the Joshua Trees and the boulders to be themselves once more. You have opened this Oasis to allow the healing waters to flow. They are all eternally grateful. Now you must return the rock with its star energy to its proper resting place. Your ring will show you where it is. It will calm down the earthquakes and allow the Earth to heal in peace."

Oh-wow! What a message! Jay-Rod said he got the same thing. But you know what? The voice in my head talked exactly the same as the man in the white suit! Where was he? I jumped up and looked around. Not inside the Oasis near the rocks. Not outside on the path. Not down by the Visitor Center. Not over by the Pinto Mountain fault scarp. I even looked up high in the palm trees just in case. (Whoa, they were really tall!) Jay-Rod had no idea what I was looking for, but he came out of the Oasis anyway.

"Look what a found by one of the rocks, Bro," he said. It was a white carnation!

Oh-man! If that didn't send chills up and down my spine! Who was that man, anyway? Could he be an Indian shaman in disguise? But he was a white man. I don't think an Indian would ever take on that disguise. Would we ever know? It reminded me of the strange prospector up at the Lost Horse Mine who had given us the information about the placer gold at Old Dale. But this man knew about Jay-Rod's buzzing rock! And Mom's Zuni ring! Did he also know about the lady in the black SUV?

We sat down on the bench again in stunned silence. Now what? We would be leaving the park in a couple of days. How could we possibly find "the proper resting place" for Jay-Rod's rock? A rock with star energy? Awesome!

Jay-Rod took the ring off from around his neck and looked at it. That ring sure had a lot to do with stars, the sun, and the moon. Just looking at it gave me a chill. There were the four black obsidian suns on the face of it on the four sides of the square stone.

Then there were tiny silver stars raised up from the setting on either side of each sun. On each end of the ring band was a half moon. Then an arrow shot out between two round "moons" toward an eight-pointed star.

We looked at it together. "What to d'ya make of it, Jay-Rod? You're the one who said the inlaid stone was a star map. Could it also be a map for this park?" It didn't seem likely that the Zunis would make a map of this park where the Serranos lived. But who knows? Anyway, it was a map of star constellations in another gallaxy, not the Earth, according to Jay-Rod.

"As above, so below," pronounced Jay-Rod in his preacher's voice. Then he continued in his own voice. "I think we should look at it from every direction and say whatever we think. Unfocus our eyes, too. Sometimes we see better that way, believe it or not."

Oh, I believed Jay-Rod, all right. He could come up with the wildest ideas that turned out to be true. So I unfocused my eyes and stared at it. "You know," I finally came out with, "I think it looks like only half a map. Those mother-of-pearl inlays seem to end at one side. If they kept on going, then they would make…" My voice trailed off. What was I trying to say?

"Omygosh!" yelled Jay-Rod. "That's it! It is only half a map! If those inlays kept going they would make the points of a five-pointed star!!!"

We ran down the path toward the Visitor Center and out to our bus. No cactus wren around this time. We hopped into the back seat, put up the folding table, got out paper and pencils and started drawing our version of a star map.

11

Star Map

Mom couldn't understand what in the world we were doing: cutting out five-pointed stars of different sizes then putting them this way and that on maps of the park. Then cheering or groaning with each one we tried. Failures, failures, all of them! It was tough going. We cut out at least a dozen paper stars of different sizes. None of them seemed to fit.

We wanted the tips of the star points to touch as many important locations in the park as possible. Then we hoped the center of the star would fall on some special new location—or an old location—or any location! That would tell us where Jay's rock's "proper resting place" should be. The centers mostly fell on mountain tops! Uuh!

Then we tried choosing an interesting location and centering the star on that. Draw yourself a five-pointed star and you'll see. We hoped the five points would then touch some other locations we knew about. That was even more discouraging. The points mostly didn't touch anything! Even when we twisted the star around pretty "vigorously," as Jay noted.

Now what? Well, we could toss up the Zuni ring, and where it landed on the park map would be the spot to deposit the rock. (My little joke.) Mom overheard us and strenuously objected to that last one. In fact she "confiscated" the ring at once, as Jay-Rod put it. (Is this getting too complicated for you? Don't worry. It was for us, too.)

"Darry, I've got it!" sang out Jay-Rod at last. And he did. Somehow he found that if you placed one of our smaller stars with the tip of its top point at the Oasis of Mara, then the tip of the left-hand point would fall on Hidden Valley, our present campsite. The tip of the right-hand point would fall on Old Dale. The tip of the bottom right-hand point would fall on

Cottonwood Visitor Center, and the tip of the bottom left-hand point would fall—over the Little San Bernadino Mountains and out of the park. (Oh, well, four out of five, at least!)

And where did the center of that star fall? Hmm. That was hard to figure out: I guess it would be in the middle of nowhere between the Geology Tour Road and the Pinto Basin Road. Was there anything at all near those roads that we hadn't seen? Hey, there's Arch Rock in the White Tank Campground! We haven't been there! Whoopee! It wasn't exactly at the center, but so what? So that is where we headed on our next drive.

Tip of the top!
Tip of the bottom!
Tip of the right and left sides!
Over the top!
Under the bottom!
Watch where our orange bus rides!
Whoopee!

You know me, but you understand that at heart I am deadly serious. No, not dead—yet . But Jay-Rod predicted I would be and him too, if I didn't keep both hands on the wheel! After I ran out of verses for my latest song, I kept up a stream of jabbering with Jay-Rod so he wouldn't feel too sad about parting with his beloved buzzing rock.

"Y'know, Jay, ol' buddy, I bet Arch Rock will end up exactly in the center of our star map after the next earthquake. Did ya ever think of that?" (Silence). I could see he wasn't in the mood for "frivolity" as he sometimes calls it. So I shut up, too, and aimed the bus for the White Tanks Campground. Arch Rock was on a nature trail that started near campsite #9.

I followed the Pinto Basin Road and made a quick left turn-off and then left again into the campground. Then I drove on around the campground to site #9 where the trail started. We pulled up and began getting our gear together for the short hike to Arch Rock. But before we could put a hand on either door handle to get out, a black SUV pulled up on one side of us. Then another black SUV pulled up on the other side. What's going on?

That lady jumped out of the one and a man out of the other. They opened both our bus doors and yelled: "Okay boys. The game's up. Get out! Let's move it!" Then they half dragged us out of the bus and pushed us against either side before we could even think of what to do.

"Where's the rock?" the man demanded. "Just give us the rock and we won't hurt you. And don't try to tell us you don't have it with you, because we know you do! C'mon, where is it?"

I tried to pull myself away from the man and get over to the other side to help my little brother. But the man had a tight grip on one arm. He shoved me back against the bus with a thump. Later Jay-Rod told me the woman was brandishing a hunting knife. Neither Jay-Rod or me were any kind of fighters. Our first defense was usually our quick wits, but it didn't work this time. They took us both by such sudden surprise we didn't know which way was up.

"Give 'em the rock, Jay-Rod," I finally managed to blurt out. "It's not worth getting hurt over. I hope they get radiation sickness from it!"

That sort of stopped them for a moment. But Jay-Rod got back in the front seat anyway. He pulled his backpack from under the seat and threw it at the lady. She caught the pack and opened it. There was the glittery rock, all right. She grabbed the rock and nodded to the man. Then dropped the empty backpack and got back into her SUV. The man let loose of me and started for the other SUV. I gave him a hard shove. He turned to hit me, I guess, but then thought better of it and got into his SUV too. Then away they roared. I picked up a stone and heaved it in their direction, but they were already gone.

"You okay, Bro?" I looked my little brother over carefully. "Did she hurt you?"

I was really shaken but he seemed fine and not even scared. Now that I looked closer I could see he was even smiling.

"They didn't get the rock," he whispered in my ear. "The stone they have is just a piece of fool's gold I picked up at Old Dale. The real rock is up in the poptop. I was just getting ready to get it when they pulled up. They'll never know the difference. What a laugh on them!"

"Jay-Rod! What a neat feat! How did you ever think of it? A dummy rock for the dummies! Fool's gold for the fools. Yippee!" Now I was back to normal, too. But Jay-Rod said he wasn't planning to fool anybody. He had just stashed the real rock up in the poptop one night, and forgot all about it till today. The piece of fool's gold was one he collected and put in his pack when I was doing my dry panning for gold at Old Dale.

But how those people found us here, we'll probably never know. Maybe they were following us all along. Maybe they overheard us talking at our campground. Maybe they even asked Mom, for all we knew. Jay-Rod thought maybe they bugged our bus, but I didn't think that was very likely. Whatever the case, we decided to keep the whole thing to ourselves. No use getting Mom upset or the park police involved. After all, we still had the rock, so it was almost like nothing ever happened.

Now Jay-Rod got the real rock out of the poptop, but before he could slip it into his backpack, I grabbed it first and looked at it closely. Yeah. It looked just like a rock. Just like I said that first day. And I didn't hear any buzzing either. Did he?

He said it was vibrating a little and put it up against my ear. "Close your other ear with your finger and see if that makes a difference." Well, sort of. I guess I could feel a faint vibration. It wouldn't give us radiation sickness, would it? Jay-Rod laughed at that. He said he was sure it wasn't uranium. After our experiences with the shaman and the deva, he felt it was some other kind of unknown mineral—maybe from another planet, or even another galaxy. Hoo-boy! My little brother!

How those SUV people knew about it was also a puzzlement, for sure. We tried for a long time to figure that one out. Maybe they were hired by someone else who had lost the rock and was trying to get it back. What would they do when they found out they had the wrong rock? Jay-Rod didn't think they would ever know the difference. By then we would have put our rock in its "proper resting place" and be long gone ourselves.

So now I placed the rock carefully back in Jay's backpack, picked up my own backpack with supplies in it, and locked the bus. Then we started down the trail to Arch Rock.

As Jay-Rod was putting on his backpack he happened to look down. There at his feet was the lady's hunting knife! Oh-wow! She must have dropped it when he threw the backpack at her. Would she be back for it? Jay-Rod doubted it. He thought she wouldn't even remember about it. It seemed to him that dropping the knife and not picking it up showed how nervous she must have been about the whole thing, too. He stashed in it his pack and we started down the trail again.

Getting to where we could see Arch Rock was a roadrunner's feather. A loop trail wound through gigantic boulders like the ones in Jumbo Rocks. And right there it was—the 25-foot arch. Arches are really cool formations, and this was a big one. But getting up under it was something else. We had to squeeze between some massive minerals to reach it, if you know what I mean. They call "boulder-scrambling."

There was no trail or any good way to go. Finally we were able to scramble up and over rocks behind the arch and then look back through it. It was about 15 feet high, but you couldn't really stand right under it since there was no platform, only piled up boulders. I wished Mom was there to sketch it.

But this didn't seem to be the place to leave Jay's rock. We decided to go on to the White Tank, a catchment basin. A dam was built across a wash in the early 1900's by a cattleman named White to catch the mountain snowmelt for his cattle. These days it's filled with sand instead of water. But it's still damp enough to attract birds and wildlife.

There's really no trail to the White Tank either. You can only reach it by boulder-scrambling for about 65 yards from the arch. First we scrunched through a narrow alley between humongous boulders. Then we came to an even larger boulder about 40 feet high. Try scrambling up that! We didn't have to. Instead we scrambled down through an alley past this boulder to another large boulder with a passage under it. By pulling ourselves through that passage we finally got to the head of the White Tank. Whew!

To us the White Tank seemed a fitting place for Jay-Rod's marvelous rock. Should we bury it in the sand or just leave it sitting on top like it was on the desert. Jay thought that whether we buried it or not it might get washed down to the actual dam and be re-buried there with sand.

Was that okay? He thought so. But maybe he should do a meditation to find out. So he did, sitting on a convenient rock.

This one went on for longer than usual, it seemed to me. Finally, before I screamed or whistled or started reciting poetry, the strangest thing happened. A little hummingbird flew over to Jay-Rod and hovered in front of his face.

Hssst! I tried to alert him. He finally opened his eyes and stared eye-to-eye with the bird. It just hovered there, never moving an inch. Was it telling him something? He wouldn't say. But he did admit that it was a "significant" sign. When I looked up the meaning of "significant" later in the dictionary, it said: "having a special, secret, or disguised meaning." Hmm. Well, if it was secret, Jay was never going to tell me. I'd have to worm it out of him. But he did agree to leave the rock on the sand in the middle of the tank.

So we did. And then another strange thing happened. As we stood there looking at that mysterious little rock sitting on top of the sand, it seemed to move. I kid you not!

It sort of wriggled and shifted itself around until it sank deeper and deeper into the sand. And then it was gone! It had buried itself! Whoa! I wanted to sneak over and see how deep it was, but Jay-Rod wouldn't let me. "Let sleeping rocks lie," was his reply.

He also said the bird was an Anna's Hummingbird, one of the scrappy little Western hummers. Finally it darted away, but then it came back and did the most peculiar thing. It flew up high above Jay-Rod and came barreling down at his head in a nose dive, suddenly turning upward in a sweep, making a sharp popping sound near his head as it made its turn. Sounded like a dive bomber breaking the sound barrier. It did that three times, and then it was gone. Hoo-boy! I thought it was going to hit him in the head for sure, but it always popped and turned up just in time. He stood stock still and never moved a muscle. Double hoo-boy!

When I told Mom afterward, she said it was a male Anna's Hummingbird doing its "pendulum display." That's what it would do during the mating season to impress a female bird. I hoped it impressed Jay-Rod. It sure was exciting to see its performance. Looked like a miniature green and red Christmas tree ornament when it hovered in front of his face. Then it turned into a tiny red-and-green missile when it dive-bombed him three times!

Mom said that Anna's are the only hummers in the country to have red crowns and red throats. But I wanted to know why the bird would do that at Jay-Rod. She said it probably knew he was an indigo. C'mon, Mom, get serious!

Instead of driving back to camp, I drove us all the way over to the Visitor Center. I wanted to buy a souvenir of some kind to remember this place by, since we were leaving in the morning. Jay-Rod said he'd wait in the bus.

I think he was still feeling fuzzy from his meditating at the White Tank. Or maybe from that bird buzzing in his face. He said the sound the bird made (not the popping) reminded him of the rock. Since the rock was buried there in the tank, I thought maybe that's what he heard.

You know, maybe the bird heard that rock, too, and just wanted to add it's own buzzing to the party. Or could the buzzing be some kind of language—maybe from another planet. Well, my off-beat ideas weren't any weirder than the other things that happened to us at Joshua Tree National Park, were they?

So I went into the Visitor Center store and yes, the strangest thing happened there too. The place was empty except for one ranger. No tourists. No other clerks. When the ranger turned to look at me I saw he was an Indian in a ranger uniform. That sort of surprised me. He could see that it did, and he began telling me all the other things Native Americans do these days—like paint pictures, build buildings, use computers, practice medicine, write books, and on and on.

Then he started telling me even stranger things—how some Indians could see things that were invisible to other people and hear things nobody else could hear. Were Indians also indigos, I wondered?

I guess he read my mind because he laughed. "We were the original indigos, only they called us "red-digos!" We both laughed.

Then he started telling me a legend about a hummingbird. Whoa! Who had mentioned hummingbirds? He said that all the birds and animals on the desert had lessons to teach people. He said hummingbirds were spirits of goodness and beauty and joy. Everywhere they went they tried to teach people and animals to do the right thing.

This is what he said. There is a story about a hummingbird and a coyote that the people tell. Once upon a time the rock people made beautiful blankets and wore them out in the fresh air and sun. Coyote came along and saw these beautiful blankets covering the rocks. He decided to take one for himself to wear as a new coat. Little Hummingbird flew over and warned him not to do it or something bad would happen. But he did it anyway. He wrapped it around himself and ran away through the rocks.

But as he traveled along he thought he heard someone coming behind him. He looked and saw a big round boulder coming after him, rumble, rumble. It was the boulder he had taken the blanket from. "Now the blanket is mine!" shouted Old Man Coyote as he ran away. Still the boulder followed him, rumble, rumble.

Then Coyote spied Mule Deer and cried, "Please help me Mule Deer. That rock is trying to crush me. You are so strong with your antlers, you could stop it." "Yes, I am stronger than any rock." So Mule Deer stood in the trail and lowered his antlers. But Old Man Rock just rolled over his antlers, crack, and went on. Now Coyote was really scared. He screamed to Bighorn Sheep that Old Man Rock was trying to crush him, and he needed help from someone very strong. "Yes, I am stronger than any rock." So Bighorn sheep lowered his head to stop the boulder. But Old Man Rock simply rolled right over his horns, crack, and went on.

Then Coyote spied Little Hummingbird again. "Please help me Little Hummingbird or Old Man Rock is going to crush me." Little Hummingbird hated to see any animal hurt, even a coyote. So she whirred her wings until she made a strong dust devil. That little tornado whirled so hard that Old Man Rock came to a stop, but right on Coyote's tail. Oow!

Little Hummingbird said, "Give back the blanket to its rightful owner. Then I will fix your tail."

He didn't want to do it, but what choice did he have? So Coyote gave back the blanket to Old Man Rock. Then Little Hummingbird whirred her wings again so hard that, crack, the rock split in two. Old Man Coyote got up, shook his tail, grabbed the blanket again, and took off. Little Hummingbird just shook her head. "That coyote will never learn."

I clapped for the ranger's story. "That's really a good one." But I wasn't sure why he was standing there in the Visitor Center telling me a story about a hummingbird. He seemed to know exactly how I felt.

"Why do you think the old people used to tell that story to the young people?" he asked me with a sly grin.

I didn't really know what to say, so I just muttered: "So they wouldn't try to take something that didn't belong to them?"

"Could be," he replied. "Or was it to teach them not to brag about their special abilities?"

Whoa! That answer hit home. Then he smiled and handed me a little woven straw hummingbird. "I know you came in here for a souvenir, so maybe this one will do." Before I could answer he extended his hand for me to shake. "Have a good one, Mr. Mighty Spiritual Being!" and he turned and went into another room.

Whee-yoo! What'd'ya say about something like that? I went outside to tell Jay-Rod about the Indian ranger. There he was twirling around in circles again in the Visitor Center courtyard with his arms straight out like helicopter blades, making whirring noises. Only I knew he wasn't being a helicopter this time. I think it was more like a "pendulum display." He finally slowed down and went in the Center to take a look. I waited in the bus. He was back before I knew it, giving me the strangest look.

"Darrell, are you all right? I didn't see any Indian ranger in the Visitor Center store. I really looked around very carefully. But there were too many people buying things for me to be comfortable."

That did it! I jumped out of the bus and went back inside to see for myself. Jay-Rod was right. The store was now full of tourists. The only rangers visible were two women clerks behind a counter. I got back in the bus without a word and just sat there.

"Hey, Bro, aren't you going to start the bus?"

Yeah, I was. But first I opened my right hand. In it was a little straw hummingbird! How d'ya explain that? Jumpin' Joshua Trees!

12

Jarod's Turn

I promised Darrell I'd let him tell our story, as he is such a great storyteller. ("You know it," as he would say.) But in the end I decided I just had to set the record straight. The trip we took to Joshua Tree National Park was the most exciting adventure I have ever been on. Something I didn't expect. I must have picked up on Darrell's feelings about deserts being boring places. Believe me, they are not. No place on Earth is really boring, you know. What makes people say things like that is the people. They make things boring, not the Earth.

Everything about the Earth and its creatures is fascinating, not boring. Who would have believed that rocks could be, too? I knew all along that rocks had life in them, but to get closely acquainted with them like I did in Joshua, really blew my mind. And the trees? I used to think palm trees were the most wonderful plants on Earth. Now I have to admit it is the Joshua Trees. I really made some close friends among the Joshua Trees there. Does that sound strange to you?

Think about it for a minute. I'll bet you have a favorite tree, too. A tree that you came to know because it grows in your yard, or because it has beautiful blossoms in the spring, or you climbed it when you were a kid. Right? That's how I feel about the Joshua Trees now. Do I have a favorite one? I'll have to admit that there are two: that thick-branched tree where the lady took my picture, (I wish she'd send me a copy!) and the scrawny tree that told me about the standing stones.

Did the trees really talk to me? You bet they did. They will talk to anyone who takes the time with them. Time is the important thing. But you have to touch them first. Put your arms around them and talk out loud to them. Sing a song or say a poem, too. Darrell's poems were so full of fun that even the trees couldn't help but feel it. Maybe your tree needs water or some kind of natural fertilizer. (No chemicals!) Give it some. Make it feel wanted and important. And don't let anybody trim its branches or cut it down. You know that trees make oxygen, don't you? The air we breathe. Why would anyone want to harm a maker of oxygen?

When I heard that the pioneers in Joshua Tree used to burn those trees at night as torches to light the way for travelers, it made me feel sick. I know there used to be hundreds more trees in Joshua Tree Park than there are today. People probably thought other ones would grow up quickly. But nothing grows quickly on a desert. Or maybe they never stopped to think at all. They never realized what a unique thing the Joshua Tree is—king of the Mohave Desert. Just like the tall saguaro cactus trees over in Arizona are kings of the Sonoran Desert. They would talk to you, too. But they're not the hugging kind of tree, if you know what I mean!

If you want a tree to talk you need to sit really close, close your eyes, and concentrate on the tree. Most people are not very good at concentrating. They keep letting other things enter their minds. If you can hold out long enough you will get some kind of signal from the tree. Maybe it will shake its leaves or sway. Keep doing these things day after day and finally you will hear something. Once you've made the connection it will be easier another time. Try it and see.

The other remarkable things in that park are the rocks—the monzo-granite boulder piles. You probably think that rocks are just rocks. Wrong. Each kind of rock is different from every other kind. And each rock of a certain kind is different from the others.

The rocks in Joshua Tree National Park have been there so long they have stored up enormous memories. I'm glad the park people recognized certain rocks because of their size or shape—or that they looked like something everyone would recognize. The rock climbers recognized them, too. The rocks they named feel good about it, but not the ones they pounded their pitons into.

Although rocks are much slower than trees, they still feel things. They will talk to people who show they like them, and who have the patience to wait. I wish the rock climbers knew that. Wouldn't it be great for them to have a conversation with their favorite rocks? Rocks like to be climbed. Did you know that? They like to feel people up against them. I wonder if any rock climber ever talked his rock? Wouldn't he be surprised if the rock answered?

Because every rock is different, some are the strong silent types, and some are real gabbers! Yes, it's true. But their talk is different than the trees. They talk with deep vibrations. You may have to translate what they say. Sounds crazy, doesn't it? But if you never tried it, how do you know? We people on Earth just take so many things for granted. We never really get to know what's going on in the natural world around us. Native Americans know. Indigo children know, too.

By the way, it's better not to call us indigos. We are children just like other children. If you have to call us something, say we're the "new" children. We came to help people understand more about themselves and their surroundings. Things are changing on the Earth—quicker than you realize, and we can help people to understand this. People need to care for each other and the Earth. No more fighting or polluting. That's why we're here: to show people how to care for one another and for the world around them.

But back to Joshua Tree National Park. Who would have believed that a national park would be set up for rocks! I know. You're going to say it was set up for the Joshua Trees. True. But the trees and boulders are partners in the high Mohave Desert. Everything is connected, you know. If the rocks weren't there, the ground squirrels and coyotes, and the rattlesnakes wouldn't be. If the trees weren't there, the birds and other plants wouldn't be.

Well, enough of my soap box lecture! You probably are more interested in what happened after Darrell's run-in with the Indian park ranger. It's hard to explain about all the beings on Earth. There are people here who aren't real people like us, you know—three-dimensional. I don't know who the Indian was, maybe a shaman or an angel. But he gave Darrell something three-dimensional: the straw hummingbird. That was real. About the man in white—who can explain him either? But he left something real behind—the white carnation. And the old prospector? Well, he gave us the directions to Old Dale, and guess what? Darrell panned out some real gold...not just a fool's gold rock like I tricked the lady with, but some tiny flakes of real gold.

He made Mom find an assay office in town. They weighed his gold and actually paid him $20 dollars! That's right. He split it with me. Mom found the hunting knife in my pack. I told her I found it at the White Tank trail. She put it away with our camping gear. She didn't have to remind me to return my rock to the park where I found it. I told her I put it back in an even better place.

What about our rock energy? Were you wondering? It's still inside us for all we know. Will it ever come out? I think it will when the time and place are right. But it doesn't bother us or make us feel sick like it did at first. Every once in awhile we smile at each other and point to our stomachs. We know what that means. We feel honored to carry the Heart Rock energy.

Have you ever heard of the word "surreal"? The dictionary says is means "unreal" "fantastic" or "having the quality of a dream." Well, I think that Joshua Tree National Park itself is a surreal place. Most people probably never experience the things that we did. That's because their minds are not as open as ours. Maybe my abilities helped open our minds to things other people never see or hear.

Anyway, the surreal-ness of the place even affected Mom. It totally changed her style of painting. When we saw the thirteen pictures she produced, we couldn't believe our eyes. They were surreal too! Darry mentioned her painting of Split Rock looking like a meteorite with lines radiating out of it. Her other rock paintings looked just as weird—almost like they were alive. She even had a rock-climber in one of them, going up without any ropes. I thought it was me at first. But then I looked closer and decided it looked more like an angel. Same thing. (Naw, that's Darrell's joke). And her Joshua Trees? They were dancing in the wind! One was even on top of a boulder!

When she showed her paintings to the clerks in the Visitor Center store, they loved them!! Yes! They wanted to take some on consignment right away. She left one, I think, but said she would have to talk to her agent about the others. They told her if she could paint rocks and trees like that, all the national park stores in California, Utah, New Mexico and Arizona would want some. They gave her an association address to contact.

Maybe best of all, they gave her the address of a children's book writer in Twenty-nine Palms, so he could see her paintings. We stopped there, and he not only fell in love with them (the paintings), but he wants her to illustrate a children's book he is doing about a rock, a coyote, and a hummingbird! In Darrell's words: I kid you not!

And guess what else? We're coming back to the desert next year—to the red rock country in Utah. If Mom gets a contract to paint rocks and desert vegetation, she may even move there. But if she doesn't, we're coming anyway. Remember, she is a petroglyph freak and Utah is petroglyph country. Mom wants to find out if I can really interpret what they say.

What a poem Darry made up when he heard that! It had more verses than "99 Bottles of Beer in the Wall"! But I liked what he said at the end best of all. In Joyce Kilmer's words: "Poems are made by fools like me/ But only God can make a tree." Thanks, God, for Joshua Trees!

Glossary

Astral body: a person's invisible bodily shape

Booby hatch: mental hospital

Camouflaged: disguised

Confiscated: seized

Culprit: a guilty person

Curse: a saying intended to cause misfortune to another

Deja-vu: seeing something for the first time, already seen earlier

Dematerialize: to take away an object's substance

Detect: discover

Doleful: mournful

Embedded: inserted into a surrounding mass

Eons: largest divisions of geologic time

Frivolity: having fun

Humungous: huge, enormous

Imperative: absolutely necessary

Joints: cactus sections

Lethargic state: the state of being drowsy or listless

Levitate: to rise or float in the air

Meditate: to engage in deep thought; to go into the mind's levels

Noctural hypothermia: below normal nighttime body temperature

One-dimensional: the first of the three dimensions; flat

Osmosis: sucking in of one thing by another

Ostentatious: showy display intended to impress others

Pendulum display: a to and fro, or up and down swinging motion

Penetrate: to pierce into something

Peruse: to examine in detail

Piton: metal spike for rock climbing

Predicament: a difficult or puzzling situation

Procure: to obtain by effort

Shaman: Indian medicine man

Surrealistic: having the quality of a dream; above realistic; fantastic

Synchronicity: a coincidence of events in time

Third degree: intensive questioning to get a needed answer

Vigorously: full of energy; forcefully

Vintage: a classic; something of quality from a past time

Bibliography

Furbish, Patty. *On Foot in Joshua Tree National Park.* Moose, WY: M.I. Adventure Publications, 2005.

Gingery, Mari. *Joshua Tree Bouldering,* Joshua Tree, CA: Quail Springs Publishing, 2000.

Keiser, James. *Joshua Tree the Complete Guide.* Destination Press, 2000.

Le Gallienne, Richard. *The Le Gallienne Book of English and American Poetry.* Garden City, NY: Garden City Publishing Company, 1925.

Patterson, Alex. *A Field Guide to Rock Art Symbols of the Greater Southwest.* Boulder, CO: Johnson Books, 1992.

Peterson, Roger Tory. *A Field Guide to Western Birds.* Boston: Houghton Mifflin, 1990.

Twain, Mark. *Roughing It.* Hartford, CT: American Publishing Company, 1872.

Readers Guide

1. What were Jarod's psychic abilities?

2. How did Darrell feel about his brother Jarod's psychic abilities? How would you feel if Jarod was your brother?

3. How did Jarod find out that the trees and rocks in the park needed help?

4. Who stole Jarod's buzzing rock? How did the boys get it back?

5. How did Jarod stop the rock from being stolen the second time?

6. What happened with the rock energy from Heart Rock?

7. What were Darrell's three wishes? What was the result of each one?

8. What was the role of their Mom's Zuni ring?

9. Who do you think the Indian ranger, the man in white, and the old prospector were?

10. How did their Mom show she was affected by the strange energies in the park?

11. How did the boys finally help the trees, rocks, and Joshua Tree National park itself?

CPSIA information can be obtained at www.ICGtesting.com
Printed in the USA
LVOW09s2322031214

417076LV00003B/5/P